DARCY

Amanda by Candice F. Ransom
Susannah by Candice F. Ransom
Elizabeth by Willo Davis Roberts
Danielle by Vivian Schurfranz
Joanna by Jane Claypool Miner
Jessica by Mary Francis Shura
Caroline by Willo Davis Roberts
Kathleen by Candice F. Ransom
Marilee by Mary Francis Shura
Laura by Vivian Schurfranz
Emily by Candice F. Ransom
Jacqueline by Jeffie Ross Gordon
Victoria by Willo Davis Roberts
Cassie by Vivian Schurfranz
Roxanne by Jane Claypool Miner
Megan by Vivian Schurfranz
Sabrina by Candice F. Ransom
Veronica by Jane Claypool Miner
Nicole by Candice F. Ransom
Julie by Vivian Schurfranz
Rachel by Vivian Schurfranz
Corey by Jane Claypool Miner
Heather by Vivian Schurfranz
Gabrielle by Mary Francis Shura
Merrie by Vivian Schurfranz
Nora by Jeffie Ross Gordon
Margaret by Jane Claypool Miner
Josie by Vivian Schurfranz
Diana by Mary Francis Shura
Renée by Vivian Schurfranz
Jennie by Jane Claypool Miner
Darcy by Mary Francis Shura

Mary Francis Shura

A SUNFIRE Book

SCHOLASTIC INC.
New York Toronto London Auckland Sydney

ISBN 0-590-42016-X

12 11 10 9 8 7 6 5 4 3 2 1 9/8 0 1 2 3 4/9

Printed in the U.S.A. 01

First Scholastic printing, August 1989

Chapter One

Wednesday, September 5, 1900

DARCY Dunlop, wearing only her ruffled cotton camisole and knee-length knickers, flipped crossly through the dress rack in her closet. "Nothing," she said. "Angela, I am telling the absolute truth. I have *nothing* to wear to my own birthday party."

Angela Morton, sitting cross-legged on Darcy's bed, laughed as she buffed her nails to the same rosy pinkness as her cheeks. "I can't believe the way you exaggerate everything, Darcy."

Darcy glared at her. "Fine best friend you are. I have this awful crisis. I am actually suffering and all you can do is criticize my style."

"Having your birthday party moved inside from the beach doesn't sound like genuine torture to me," Angela admitted.

"It does to me," Darcy said. "Mostly I just can't

believe it's happening. I've been planning this party and looking forward to it all summer. I'm only going to turn sixteen once in my entire life. Then Papa decides to *ruin* my sixteenth birthday before it even starts. Who ever heard of having an inside dancing party on a hot September night?"

"I imagine it's been done," Angela protested mildly. "Besides, you know your father wouldn't ask you to do this unless he felt the weather was really chancy."

"Weather! If just once Papa would let the weather happen on its own without worrying about it for days in advance."

"He loves you too much to have you take chances," Angela said quietly.

"I don't know why he always has to show his love by worrying. Him and his weather! If I had my way, I'd break every barometer in Texas. That's the only way I can think of to keep him from checking one every hour on the hour."

"What makes you think your father is the only one who acts that way? My father's just as bad, and he's in the construction business. If he made his living from a schooner like your father's *Sojourner*, I bet he'd be twice as bad. And they're not alone, either. The men here in Galveston only know two things to talk about — weather and building a seawall along the gulf."

Darcy glanced over at her. "I'll say this for you. You stick up for *some* of your friends."

"I like your father," Angela said. "I will admit that this decision of his was rather sudden. Just yesterday you were still talking about a beach party."

"Thank you for that much understanding," Darcy said, her dark eyes snapping with annoyance. "It wasn't sudden. It was, as Mrs. Turner would say, a bolt out of the blue. Hildy wasn't even expecting him for lunch when he came flying in here this noon. You know how he is. Every time he gets off that ship of his, he manages to go by the Levy Building to check with the weather bureau. The minute he left there today he came straight home and announced we'd have to move my beach party indoors. Ruining it!"

When Angela fell silent, Darcy knew what her friend was thinking. Angela's own mother had been deathly afraid of storms herself since the hurricane four years before in which she had nearly been killed by an uprooted tree. Now Angela would spring to Darcy's father's defense again, making Darcy feel like an absolute worm for not getting along any better than she did with her father. But Angela's father, Mr. Morton, was a big, genial man, always smiling and laughing. Angela hadn't ever lived with a father who went around with a long face or sat silent for hours at a time, staring off at nothing.

Her father hadn't always been that way. Sometimes Darcy thought her father had buried the habit of laughter with his gay young wife. Didn't he realize she missed her mother as much as he did? And that the last thing her mother would want was for them to be cool and distant to each other?

"Mr. Cline must have really scared him," Angela said thoughtfully.

Darcy recalled the exact terms her father had used. "This really started yesterday when Mr. Cline told him about a 'tropical disturbance' moving northward across Cuba. Today at noon he told Papa they had issued shipping warnings down at Key West."

"No wonder your father worries so much about reports like that. After all, he has to watch for storms way out at sea as well as those that hit our coastline."

Darcy grimaced but said nothing, knowing that her friend was right. Galveston Island lay between the Gulf of Mexico and Galveston Bay. As such, it had suffered more than its share of ferocious tropical hurricanes. Since it was also the fourth largest city in Texas and a major shipping port, almost all the seafaring men like her father had lost at least one craft to twenty-foot waves that came crashing in when a storm struck in the open sea.

Darcy had heard stories of hurricanes all her life. She even vaguely remembered the hurricane of 1887, the year she was three. Actually the storm hadn't survived so much in her memory as it had haunted her dreams. For years afterward she had wakened trembling from nightmares in which the howling winds and walls of black water had hammered against the upper stories of their house. It had ripped away the balconies and shutters and snaked in hungry, licking streams across the floor of her mother's bedroom.

Darcy tugged a rose-colored shirtwaist dress from her closet and frowned. But Angela dropped the ivory-backed buffer and jumped from the bed to come stand beside Darcy at the full-length mirror.

"What I wouldn't give to be able to wear that color!" She took Darcy's dress and pressed it against herself, setting one foot forward as if she were a model posing for a picture in *The Ladies Home Journal*. When she giggled, Darcy joined in. Angela was a full three inches taller than Darcy and solidly built besides. The dress barely covered Angela's body. Worse than that, Angela, with her pale red curls and florid complexion, became all one color with the dress held against her. "See? All I need is pink eyes and I would disappear. But look at you!"

Darcy didn't want to look at herself. She knew the color was perfect for her fair complexion and black hair. She knew it even brightened her face without her having to slap or pinch her cheeks.

Angela sighed. "I don't care if that S-curve style is the latest thing — I hate it. No style is worth lacing your stomach to your backbone in an old, stiff corset."

When she tossed the dress across the bed, Darcy

nodded and glared at it. "You know it's going to be hot on Friday night, too hot to be indoors bundled in a ton of clothes. I'll sweat like a stevedore, you wait and see. Anyway, everyone has seen this stupid dress already."

"Perspire," Angela corrected her, settling back down on Darcy's bed. "Make up your mind. Are you mad because you hate being dressed up or because you don't have anything new?"

"I *have* something new," Darcy reminded her. "My new beach costume will be totally wasted. I've never had one I paid so much for or that looked so good on me. And come on, admit it, Angela, beach parties are ever so much more fun, with the food on long tables and the music playing over the sound of the surf."

She slumped on the bed beside Angela, staring off into space. The beach costume she had bought especially for this party was in the very latest style, serge, with a very full skirt and knickers with ruffles at her knees. The shoes even laced halfway up her calves, making her look like a dancer.

"If you're thinking about my cousin Michael seeing you in your new outfit, you could always wear it tomorrow," Angela suggested in a sly, soft voice.

Angela's words caught Darcy off guard. She *had* been wondering if Michael Stephens would admire her in her new bathing outfit. But it was so annoying to have anyone read her mind that Darcy whirled on her.

"You and your Michael! That's all you think of anymore. I have to tell you, Angela Morton, that just because Michael Stephens is your cousin doesn't make him anyone special to me. In fact, he's not only a Yankee, he's rude."

"He's *not* rude," Angela protested, rising swiftly to her cousin's defense. "He just speaks his mind, that's all. And if you don't think he's special, you're all by yourself. Every other girl in Galveston has been making calf's eyes at him since the day he got here. You watch. A lot of tears are going to flow next week if he decides to go back and work in New England instead of staying here to join my father's company."

This talk of Michael's leaving brought Darcy up short. And that was ridiculous because she had been determined not to like him from the first. Angela had spoiled him for Darcy before he even got there. She had raved on and on about this wonderful cousin of hers who had finished his engineer's training at the youngest age ever. She had bragged about his brains, his personality, and his looks so much that the very name "Michael" was enough to turn Darcy's stomach. On top of that, Angela must have told Darcy a million times how much she was going to like him. Well, she *hadn't* liked him when he came and she still didn't.

But Angela was right about one thing. Michael Stephens had caused an undue amount of stir in the three weeks since he had come to visit the Morton family. And he was handsome enough, if you liked that burnished golden look that blond men get when they spend a lot of time in the sun. His manners, most of the time, were surprisingly gallant and he *did* have some charming habits. He had a way of listening when she spoke which made whatever she said feel wonderfully important. But his curiosity was somehow upsetting. It was understandable that he would be interested in Galveston, since he was thinking about making his home there. But Michael's curiosity was so probing that he sometimes made Darcy feel as if all of them were freaks in a circus to him.

Darcy wanted to ask why he was in such a hurry to leave when he hadn't even been in Galveston a month. Instead, she kept her question to herself. The *last* thing she wanted was for Angela to think she would be among those crying calves. But Angela's silence made Darcy wish she hadn't flown off like that at her. Her friend generally spoke the truth whether Darcy wanted to hear it or not.

In any case, a person certainly couldn't be held accountable for their relatives. Thank goodness for that, too. If Darcy herself had to be responsible for her fifteen-year-old cousin Rose, she would literally die. At the thought of Rose, she groaned. "I know as sure as I'm standing here that Rose will wear this color to my party. Aunt Julie always buys Rose clothes to match her name. She'll have trouble keeping her sash tied and her hair will look like old laundry after the first two dances. So this dress is out!"

"I *knew* something was different," Angela said. "This is the first private visit we've had since your cousin came. Where is she, anyway?"

Darcy shrugged. "She is a strange one. She's wild about little kids, you know. She made friends with one of the sisters at St. Mary's Orphanage. The sister told Rose she could come any time she wanted, to play games and read books to the little kids. Rose left here early with a basket of fruit and balls and old toys jumbled in together."

Darcy shook her head but Angela laughed. "Rose may be strange, but she is fun to be around."

Darcy couldn't argue with that. Rose *was* fun. But although she was only a few months younger than Darcy, she seemed like an overgrown child. Each summer she spent a month with Darcy and her father. Every year Darcy hoped Rose would have gotten herself a little more under control before she came.

There was simply no one in the world like Rose. She lost all her belongings. Her parcels came open on the public sidewalks. Her dresses came unhooked. Her packing was never done on time. She made appointments for the wrong day, and forgot people's names and addressed them wrongly. But at least her sense of humor extended to herself; she often collapsed into laughter without warning, usually spilling tea down the front of her clothing. Stray animals followed her. She wiped the noses of grubby urchins on the street and started up lengthy conversations with total strangers. She was as charming and warmhearted as she was disorganized, and quite embarrassing to introduce to strangers.

Angela rose and stretched. "I probably should be getting on home. The afternoon's almost over. You will be at the beach tomorrow as usual, won't you?"

Darcy made a face and shook her head. "Thanks to Papa, that's out, too. I can't possibly get away to go tomorrow. Changing my party from the beach to the house means a lot of extra work for everyone. I promised Hildy I'd stay home and help or run errands if she needed anything."

Another awkward silence fell. In the first few anguished months after Darcy's mother died of yellow fever, she was sure she would never be able to think of her mother without tears. She had learned to manage her grief with time. Although she was often struck with swift, unbearable pain, she had accepted the loss of her mother in a way that Angela never had. Maybe this was because of Angela's own mother's brush with death, but anything that reminded Angela of Darcy's mother sent Angela into silent grief. Just being reminded that Darcy, with only Hildy the housekeeper to help her, was responsible as mistress of her father's house had filled Angela's eyes with tears.

Darcy broke her silence. "It's not all that bad, Angie. I don't mind working with Hildy."

"But the beach is a bore without you!" Angela wailed. "I guess that means your cousin Rose will have to stay home and help, too. You two are always the life of the party — one way or another."

"She'll come with you if I have to push her," Darcy said. "That girl is such a jinx that even Hildy starts dropping things when she's around."

Angela chuckled. "Well, I'm glad she'll come even though I'll miss you. And Michael will miss you, too," she added slyly. "Although Alex will be delighted you're not there."

"What a thing to say!" Darcy protested. "Why should Alex not want me there? Alex is always glad to see me."

"That's exactly what I mean. Alex is glad to see you but not to have you in the company of Michael. If Alex Turner had his way, he would hide you away in a dark closet somewhere until Michael leaves. He blazes with jealousy every time Michael glances your way!"

Darcy shook her head in mock despair. What a romantic Angela was! She could find drama and tearful sentiment in the simplest exchange of glances. Alex blazing? The thought almost made her giggle. "What a steamy little mind you have, Angela. You blow everything up out of proportion," Darcy said. "You know Alex Turner and I have been friends forever."

"Friends!" Angela scoffed. "He's crazy about you and we both know it. He looks daggers at Michael every time he gets near you. I wouldn't be surprised if he sends up flares if Michael decides to cast his lot in the East. Look at how his mother treats you. She acts as if she were already your mother-in-law."

Darcy turned back to the closet restlessly. Alex Turner *had* been her friend forever and she was fond of him. She was even comfortable with him most of the time, except when he was angry and surly about something.

Mrs. Turner was the problem. She was a terribly stuffy woman with beady black eyes so small and watchful that they made Darcy itch. She and Angela privately laughed at the way Mrs. Turner talked. She never sounded as if she made up her own sentences. She either seemed to be quoting from an etiquette book or using the most hackneyed cliché in the world to express herself.

Darcy could have put up with all that. What she couldn't stand was the way Mrs. Turner had pressed herself on the Dunlop household since Darcy's mother had died. Darcy had never felt that Alex's mother and her own had been *that* close while her mother lived, but Mrs. Turner gave everyone the impression they had been bosom friends. She was forever bringing cakes or cookies over, or dropping in and offering to help with things that Darcy and Hildy could easily handle on their own.

Hildy said that Mrs. Turner just plain didn't have enough business of her own to mind. Her big house on Broadway crawled with servants. She had only Alex to worry about now that she was widowed.

Darcy knew she *should* feel grateful for the woman's concern but it was tiresome to have her pop up like a toadstool every time Darcy turned around.

Even with her head buried in the closet again, Darcy heard her terrier, Buffy, barking as he raced up the stairs. As she turned to go let him in, Hildy opened the door. Hildy stood speechless, blinking at Darcy in astonishment.

"What is on your mind, child?" she cried. "Put on some decent clothes this minute." Buffy, excited by Hildy's tone, raced around Hildy, yipping happily. Without waiting for Darcy's response, Hildy turned on Buffy. "Enough of that, young man!"

Buffy skidded to a halt and sat wagging with apology. When Angela exploded with giggles, even Hildy realized how absurd the scene was. She turned and smiled at Angela. "You're the one I really came up here to see, Miss Angela. Your cousin's below stairs. He asked if he could please speak with you and Miss Darcy."

This time Darcy herself gasped and covered her camisole with her crossed arms as if Michael himself had appeared right there in her room.

"That's great!" Angela said, leaping to her feet. "I wonder what Michael has planned for us." She glanced at Darcy. "I'll go on down. But hurry!"

"She's not going anywhere dressed like that!" Hildy said quickly, glaring at her mistress.

"I know," Darcy told her. "You go on down with Angela. I promise to hurry."

Darcy stared at the door Hildy pulled shut behind

her. What in the world was happening to her? Was she becoming impossible to please? She was thrilled at the thought that Michael wanted to talk to her. At the same time, she felt curiously insulted that he felt he could come like that — without an appointment — and expect her to greet him warmly.

"Hurry!" Angela called from the stairs, startling her from her reverie.

Chapter Two

Wednesday, September 5, 1900

AGAIN Darcy was torn two ways. Her impulse was to get dressed as quickly as she could and dance downstairs to join Angela and Michael with all the high anticipation she felt. On the other hand, it was unseemly to let any young man know how eager you felt to share his company.

"Good grief!" she muttered. "I sound exactly like Mrs. Turner!"

Who cared about unseemly anyway? The afternoon was almost over. If Michael had thought of some entertainment for them, they had little enough time for it before it would be suppertime. She lifted the rose dress from the bed and studied it critically. Did she dare put it on without a corset? It took forever to lace herself into one of the silly things, and besides, they were hot.

Darcy shrugged and wriggled into the dress. Her fingers were unusually awkward with the long row of tiny pearl buttons. What was the matter with her? Having a young man call was not so rare an event. Alex came all the time — to take her out driving, to the Opera House with his mother as chaperone, and sometimes only to visit and enjoy music with her. His visits never made her fingers turn to thumbs or gave her trouble breathing.

Once in the dress, she stood and twisted to see herself in the long mirror. It looked fine. After all, since she didn't have a big, thick waist anyway, who was going to notice?

There was no way she could hurry her hair; there was too much of it and it was far too curly and unruly. She tugged furiously at the curls that hung down her back, remembering what Angela had said about Alex being jealous.

Had Alex been behaving differently since Michael came? She was embarrassed to admit that she hadn't noticed. That in itself was a bad sign. As for what she had said about Mrs. Turner already acting like a mother-in-law, that was really ridiculous. She was far too young to think about marriage to anyone, much less with Alex, who in many ways seemed much younger than his eighteen years.

Her hair put up a good fight, but so did Darcy. She finally twisted it so fiercely that it gave up and became a flattened column up the back of her head. She would pay for this later when Hildy tugged and pulled the tangles out, but it had to do for now. She stuck enough horn pins into it to keep it from tumbling down, then brushed out the fine fringe of dark curls around her face and started downstairs.

Michael certainly looked fine enough. He was wearing cycling clothes, which made Darcy feel terribly overdressed. How tall and fashionable he looked in his tweed knickers with a matching jacket and cap. He was obviously in high spirits and his broad smile was somehow mischievous.

"Forgive my clothes," he said, dismissing them with a wave. "I was out bicycling when the wind actually took after me, trying to blow me over." He smiled at Darcy. "I asked myself what possible use there was for a wind like that. Quick, who has the answer?"

"Blowing people off their bikes," Angela suggested.

"Go to the foot of the class," he said with the frown of a stern schoolmaster. "And you, young lady?"

Darcy giggled. "You could always go fly a kite," she suggested.

His astonishment *looked* genuine. "Amazing!" he said. "But then I reflected that flying a kite alone was a sorry way to have fun. I asked myself where I could find two lovely ladies to do it with me." His glance at Darcy was a playful question.

Angela shook her head. "Flying kites isn't as

much fun as it used to be before they started putting all those poles up for electricity and telephones and all."

"Angie," he protested. "Don't be a spoilsport! I brought the buggy so we could get away from all that. I thought we'd go down to Fort Point. There's always a breeze there across from Pelican Island. You can even choose which kite you want. I brought three."

"You did think of everything," Darcy said. "Come on, Angela, doesn't that sound like fun?" She hadn't flown a kite in years, not since her mother's death. But she had loved it then, running with the kite string feeding up into the sky among the gulls, her hair loose and her roomy cotton smock billowing behind her. Just thinking of kite flying made her mother's laughter echo in her mind.

Then she hesitated, looking down at the hateful rose dress. So what if she ruined it, running through the prickly bushes? So what if she did? The very thought of battling the wind gave her a shiver of delight. And this would be the last time she flew a kite before she was sixteen.

"I'd love it myself," she said, with a pleading glance at Angela.

Angela rose and sighed. "You convinced me. Freckles, here I come."

"Freckles," Hildy echoed from the doorway. She disappeared and returned almost immediately with straw hats in one hand and a ruffled parasol in the other. "The sun is still blazing," she said sternly, handing each girl a hat.

Michael waited indulgently until both hats were tied in place, then opened the front door with a flourish.

Hildy came out on the porch as they started down the front walk. "Darcy," she protested. "Come back here! You must take a parasol."

"With a kite?" Michael asked, his voice rising. The picture was enough to start Darcy giggling. With her broad-brimmed hat, her kite and her parasol she might well take off and fly. Even Hildy laughed at his blank stare of disbelief at the idea.

"We won't be too long," he called back, his hand at Darcy's elbow. "And anyway, Hildy, your Darcy can outrun the sun."

Michael was holding his hand to help Angela step up into the surrey when a buggy pulled in behind his. The smart-stepping bay horse danced to a stop.

Darcy recognized the Turner phaeton instantly. She paused, her heart sinking. What was Alex thinking of, coming by like this without making arrangements in advance? But he was not alone. She might have known, his mother was along!

Alex took his mother's hand as she stepped down. Although Alex's father had been dead for several years, Mrs. Turner had never come out of mourning clothes. She was immaculate in a black silk walking suit with a matching hat. The only touch of color was a ruffle of cream lace caught with a cameo pin at her throat. She looked very elegant and *very* disapproving.

"Darcy," Mrs. Turner cried, approaching swiftly to offer her cheek for a kiss. "You must forgive my thoughtlessness in not sending word that I wanted to see you."

Darcy nodded, hoping this would pass for forgiveness. What was the proper etiquette for such a situation, anyway? Only a blind person could fail to see that this arrival had delayed the departure of the hostess. For a crazy moment she thought Mrs. Turner might quote the proper rule to give her some guidance. Instead, the woman went right on as if Angela and Michael and the buggy bristling with kites were invisible.

"I just heard of the change in plans for your birthday party. As a hostess myself, I know how much trouble any last-minute change in arrangements can cause. I had Alex bring me right over to let you and Hildy know that my house is at your service."

"Your house?" Darcy asked, confused.

"We have the ballroom, you know. It would be perfect for your event."

"But the guests are coming here," Darcy said.

Mrs. Turner fluttered her leather-gloved hands. "I find that no impediment. I'll simply post a servant at the gate to direct your guests on."

She paused, glancing down at Darcy's dress. Darcy felt the red rise to her cheeks. Mrs. Turner was the kind to have an eagle eye for whether someone was wearing a corset or not. The older woman's eyes widened in shocked astonishment, confirming Darcy's fear.

Hildy, bless her, came to Darcy's rescue, descending the stairs at twice her normal speed. She even spoke to Mrs. Turner too rapidly to be interrupted. "How good of you to offer, Mrs. Turner," she said, "but I am sure the captain wouldn't hear of such a change. All the arrangements have been made. Miss Darcy and I have everything under complete control."

Darcy dropped her eyes to hide her amusement. Was this the same Hildy who had made a two-page list of things she and Darcy had to get done in the next two days?

Mrs. Turner, her eyes still straying thoughtfully up and down Darcy's figure, made a helpless gesture with both hands. "I wish I could speak to Captain Dunlop myself. I'm sure he wants only the best for Darcy."

Darcy didn't dare look at Hildy, knowing that if Mrs. Turner had *tried*, she couldn't have come up with anything that would inflame Hildy more than those words.

Hildy, suddenly a good two inches taller, looked Mrs. Turner straight in the eye. "The captain feels that he *is* providing Miss Darcy with the best," she said smoothly. "But we do thank you for your generous offer."

"Just anything we can do to help," Mrs. Turner went on swiftly, her face suddenly a little flushed. "My cook is excellent. Perhaps more servants?"

Hildy's gray eyes had turned to steel. "We do thank you for your generous offer," she repeated.

In the pause that followed, Hildy's tone turned gentle. "Now if you will excuse these young people. Miss Darcy has worked very hard on her party arrangements, and I feel she needs a bit of relaxation. I *insisted* that she fly off with her friends for a bit of fun with their kites. Again, we do thank you, don't we, Miss Darcy?"

"It was lovely of you," Darcy murmured, trying to avoid Alex's eyes. She knew him too well. She had been with him before when his mother's presumptions had wounded people's feelings. Inside he must be dying with embarrassment. Even as she ached for him, he spoke her name quietly.

She looked up to realize that she had been wrong. Alex hadn't been thinking about Hildy's feelings or her own. He had only been thinking of himself. His eyes were stormy and the very angle of his handsome head betrayed his fury.

The intensity of Alex's passion had scared her before, but he had never looked this glowering. She knew in her heart that Alex would never be cruel in any rough physical way, but when he was angry he said cruel things that no amount of apology could ever erase.

"Look at you," he said to her, his tone scathing but his voice too low to be heard by the others. "Running after that Yankee masher like every other addlepated nitwit in town. I thought better of you, Darcy, I really did."

She caught her breath. Not even her own father ever called her down like that! Too shocked to think of any sensible reply, she forced herself to meet his gaze. "Is it possible that you have been wrong?" she asked quietly. Then, without meaning to, she added, "As if I had asked your opinion."

Mrs. Turner, apparently accepting her ungracious defeat, turned to Darcy again. "You are carrying a parasol, aren't you, Darcy?" she asked, her face seamed with disapproval.

"With a kite?" Hildy asked, miraculously echoing Michael's incredulous tone. "My goodness, the child would fly."

When Alex had restored his mother to the embossed leather seat of her rig, Michael drove off. When they were safely out of hearing distance, Angela collapsed in helpless giggles. "I adore that Hildy," she said. "I simply adore her!"

"Which is more than I can say for your burly friend," Michael told Darcy over his shoulder. "He's the prince of the scowlers, that one."

"Only to you," Angela said.

Michael turned to stare at Angela thoughtfully before turning back to Darcy. "Do you and Mr. Snarly have some sort of arrangement I don't know about?" he asked.

"Michael!" Angela gasped. "No wonder Darcy thinks you're a rude Yankee! What a thing to ask a girl!"

"It's a perfectly logical question," Michael protested.

Darcy said, "Well, since you've asked, the answer is no."

He smiled broadly, a wonderfully satisfied smile that wrinkled the edges of his eyes and showed his remarkably white teeth. "Now *that's* good news! On to the kites!" With that, he slapped the reins across the back of his horse.

Darcy wilted inside her corsetless dress, still trembling from the disapproval in Mrs. Turner's eyes and Alex's fury. Would her mother have thought her a loose woman to go kite flying without a corset? What would her mother have said about Alex's possessive attitude? She couldn't help wondering. Neither could she help feeling lonely and abandoned that she had no one — no one in her family to share her doubts and dreams with. How could she grow up like this, with only a father who was solemn and sad and buried in business, and Hildy, who had been there when she was born and loved her too much to think straight? Every day that she got closer to being sixteen, she liked it less.

Then Michael's voice broke into her thoughts. He was singing, almost shouting really, a crazy nautical ballad Darcy had learned from a carefree cabin boy on the *Sojourner*. She grinned, remembering how she had stood on deck between her mother and father, all three of them singing the words at the top of their lungs, just as Michael was doing.

The breeze blew sweetly salted off the gulf and gulls swung overhead, pipping complaint. A low-flying pelican, its pouch swollen with fish, sailed past them, moving toward the island where the great birds bred and raised their young. Without even meaning to, Darcy began to hum and then to sing along with Michael and Angela, keeping time to the brisk clopping of the horse's hooves.

Chapter Three

Thursday, September 6, 1900

DARCY awoke to the clatter of Rose banging about in the guest bedroom next to her own. She sighed and turned over, trying to shut out the sound. Rose was talking to someone, her voice rising and falling happily. Then came a sharp bark and Darcy grinned. Buffy adored Rose, who treated him as if he were a clever child instead of a spoiled Scottish terrier.

Darcy not only loved Rose — one was *supposed* to love one's relatives — but she liked her most of the time as well. Occasionally Darcy even envied her. For all her awkwardness, Rose was talented, having inherited the musical ability that had passed Darcy right by. Rose brought tears to Darcy's eyes when she played the piano. Once there, Rose's expression became intense and unsmiling and the keys, which only produced sharps and flats at Darcy's touch, made swirling magic that tugged at Darcy's heart. Rose's voice had a wonderful lilt to it, too, just like Aunt Julie's and Darcy's own mother's voice had had. No one ever guessed that her mother and her Aunt Julie were sisters until they spoke or began to play the piano.

Rose might have inherited the lilt but she hadn't been born with the natural grace of either her mother or Darcy. Rose rapped on the door, then swung it open, rattling the pictures on the opposite wall. Buffy charged in with her, raced around the bed, then jumped onto the foot of it to sit wagging happily.

Rose looked down at Darcy and chuckled softly.

"Hildy told me you went out kite flying without covering your face," she said, that amused lilt lightening her words. "She was right. You *did* get some sun on your face."

Rose plopped onto the side of Darcy's bed. She would have crunched Darcy's left leg if her words hadn't sent Darcy flying out of bed and across the room to the mirror.

"Not freckles," Darcy wailed. "Please tell me no freckles."

"Not a sign," Rose said genially. Then she laughed. "I would look like a Dalmatian pup if I tried that. You only have a nice pink on your cheeks. Personally, I think it's becoming."

Darcy, staring hard at herself, agreed silently. She also appreciated Rose's tact in not mentioning that her nose was every bit as pink as her cheeks.

"Are you early or am I late?" Darcy asked, splashing her face with cold water and groping at the rack by the washstand for a towel.

"We're both just right," Rose told her. "Uncle's not down yet but the bacon smells scrumptious."

"And the weather?" Darcy asked, catching her hair back with a ribbon.

"Beautiful as always," Rose said wistfully. "Clouds like towers and the gulf is that cucumber-green today." Her voice took on a yearning note. "I don't know how Mama can expect you to leave a place this wonderful to come and live with us in an old, dull, flat town like Houston. But it would sure be wonderful. It would be like getting a sister as a present."

Darcy joined her cousin at the window. The weather indeed looked beautiful and so did the view of Galveston spreading before her. Between her window and the gulf stretched block after block of fine, imposing houses much like their own. The sun glistened on their reddish slate roofs and every yard boasted huge oleanders, blooming masses of rose and white in between the dark live oak trees and swaying palms.

But the gulf was the true wonder. The long curving line of white beach was lace-trimmed with foam. Its horizon swayed with the masts of distant ships. Darcy fought a sudden rising anger at her father. Storm indeed! Why couldn't he *wait* for weather to happen instead of always borrowing trouble?

Rose glanced over, her expression timid. "What do you think, Darcy? Will Uncle decide to let you come and live with us and go to school? We'd *really* love to have you."

Darcy hugged Rose. "I know you would. And it's really flattering that you and your folks want me. But I really haven't the vaguest idea what Papa will decide. I'm making a point of not letting myself think about it. School doesn't start here until the first of October. I'm sure he'll make a decision by then."

"But you would *like* to come, wouldn't you?" Rose asked, her eyes full on Darcy's face.

"You're sweet, Rose. And your mother is sweet to want me to come and live with you. But really and truly, I'm trying not to think about her invitation until Papa makes up his mind."

Buffy heard Hildy first. He raced to the door and began to whimper and scratch at it before Darcy heard Hildy calling. Darcy was grateful to have the conversation interrupted. "You start on," she told Rose. "I'll be right along."

Darcy wiggled into her cotton morning dress with a sigh. She had told Rose the truth. She *did* try with all her might not to decide how she felt about going to live with her aunt's family and finish her schooling in Houston. It made very good sense, now that she would be sixteen, to live in a house with a regular family. And certainly it would be gayer and more fun. Darcy had really given up on her father ever becoming his old laughing, playful self again.

Sometimes she felt that she could disappear into thin air and he wouldn't notice she was missing for a long time.

She had told Rose over and over that she wasn't letting herself think about her father's decision. There was more to it than that. She couldn't really face in her own mind how it would be to leave her father, and Hildy, and her friends, and the city she loved.

And the restless majesty of the gulf.

She stepped to the window for one more swift glance at the day. Rose was right. The clouds rose in pillars like towers, like immense ships in full, billowing sail.

Houston was hot and flat and muggy and the air in the streets smelled like horses.

Her father had started eating his breakfast without waiting for her. Darcy slipped into her seat just as Rose managed her first public accident of the day. As she lifted her napkin it caught on her water goblet, spilling it down her front in a torrent. Instead of leaping to her feet, as Darcy would have done, she only gasped with a little intake of breath and glanced guiltily at her uncle. "Oh! I am sorry." She took the napkin Darcy offered and dabbed ineffectually at her lap.

His glance was indulgent. "At least it wasn't honey. You may be excused to go change, my dear. Accidents will happen."

Rose giggled at her uncle's joke and slid from her chair to run upstairs. Darcy felt strange. In the old days, her father had teased her the way he had just teased Rose. This wasn't the first time she'd watched these jesting exchanges between her father and Rose with a twinge of envy.

Did he just feel lighthearted around Rose or was Darcy herself doing something that kept him from being comfortable and playful with her?

She felt his glance and looked up at him. "And how is my almost-grown-up girl this morning?" he asked.

The tenderness in his voice brought a quick pain to her throat. "Fine, Papa," she said, keeping her voice carefully level. "It's a lovely day."

The minute her words were out, she regretted them. He would think she was hitting out at him about changing the party plans. When his eyes lingered on hers a little sadly she knew she was right. His tone was mixed — half apology and half defensiveness. "I know you feel that I've spoiled your birthday, Darcy, but I really had no choice. I've checked with Isaac Cline already this morning. The storm is still moving. Its eye is only a little northwest of Key West. It could go anywhere from there."

Hildy came in with a basket of fresh, fragrant biscuits as he spoke. Darcy felt Hildy's eyes on her and stopped the sharp words in her throat. He'd said it himself. The storm could go anywhere. Why did he have to decide it would swing around in its big counterclockwise movement and aim straight for her birthday party?

Then Rose came back downstairs, and the awkward silence was over. Silence seldom survived Rose by more than a split second or two. Rose was full of stories about the children at the orphanage, especially a rowdy little four-year-old boy who could outrun everyone at the place. And did, especially at bath time. For a moment Darcy even thought her father might laugh at Rose's description of one of the sisters holding her skirts up and chasing the little rascal. By the time Darcy had her anger under control, her father had risen, touched both girls' foreheads with kisses and left for the harbor.

Darcy barely listened to Rose's chatter as they sorted silver and set out the linen napkins for the party. Her mind kept going back to the wonderful two hours she had spent with Angela and Michael down at Fort Point. It made her feel strangely giddy to remember Michael's laughter, the way his eyes crinkled when he smiled at her. And he had smiled at her a lot. She told herself sternly that she must not let herself take his treatment of her personally. He was a flirt, a masher as Alex had called him, and she would be an absolute ninny to think he really liked her.

In fact, as she thought of it, she began to feel cross and pettish. It was mean of him to treat her so gallantly when he probably didn't care at all. He must be laughing up his well-tailored eastern sleeves at what fools he was making of a bunch of little Texas girls.

While Darcy changed into street clothes to go shopping in the Strand, Rose left to get dressed to meet Angela and the others at the beach. Darcy was through first.

Rose came down the stairs looking for all in the world like pictures of the White Queen in *Alice in Wonderland.* Her fair hair had escaped in cottony tendrils from under the ruffles of her white cap, which was a little askew over her left ear. Her pink-and-white-checked cotton bathing costume was trimmed with dark pink bows at the neck and waist. Her sash had already become untied to trail after her down the stairs. She was carrying a parasol, a set of sand tools, and something that looked like a fringed shawl. Since she couldn't possibly see the stairs, she felt her way carefully with one slipper after another, all the time giggling happily at her own predicament.

She was only two or three steps from the bottom when the inevitable happened. She tripped on her sash, squealed, threw her arms up and tumbled.

Darcy had felt the fall coming. She leaped across the foyer and caught Rose around the waist before she fell flat on the polished parquet floor. She braced her cousin a minute while the sand tools clattered down the hall. Her parasol drifted lazily down to land on the rug just inside the parlor.

Hildy appeared, wide-eyed, at the door. "Nothing

hurt?" she asked, relaxing when she saw Rose giggle as she clung to Darcy.

"Only my dignity," Rose laughed. "And there's little enough of *that* to worry about."

Darcy watched, with crossed fingers, Rose start off to the beach. If she could get there safely, Angela would look after her. From the porch the surf sounded louder than usual. She frowned. Strong waves meant strong riptides that would drag an unwary swimmer out into the depths. Would Rose know enough to swim parallel to such a tide to break free of its grip?

Since worrying wasn't going to help, she closed the door and went to the kitchen for the shopping list.

Hildy was fond of gray. Her dress was a faint pearl shade that matched her hair. She stood solidly by the counter, with a massive cleaver dancing up and down in her right hand. When she glanced up, Darcy saw that her lips were tight with disapproval.

"Something wrong?" Darcy asked, studying Hildy's usually genial face. Hildy didn't even look up. She only shook a curly gray strand of hair from her forehead and went on chopping the poached chicken breast on the breadboard.

"If you don't know, I can't tell you," Hildy said tersely. "The list is there with the money your papa left."

She was obviously trying to hold her tongue. Predictably it got away from her. After the briefest pause she spoke again, having to lift her voice above the steady, angry chopping of her busy cleaver. "What other father opens his purse to a child the way yours does? That man thinks nothing is too good for his Darcy. Look at you, the finest clothes, piano study and art lessons besides. How many girls you know have closets in their rooms, the way this town taxes a householder for every room — even closets? But can you be half civil to him long enough for him to enjoy a good breakfast?"

Darcy felt a cold chill down her spine. Don't say it, Hildy, Darcy pleaded silently. Don't ask me what my mother would think of how I'm acting. But Hildy shut her lips tight and carried the heaping bowl of delicate chicken to the icebox.

"This is a very long list," Darcy said, studying it.

"Peter will drive you. Your papa had him hitch the buggy for you before he left. It'll hold all that and more," Hildy said. "And there's a storm coming."

Peter was quiet on the ride across town. He hummed a little to himself, clucking now and then to the horse, Jemmy. Peter was a comfortable man to be with, a small, wiry man who had been a sailor before his leg was nearly twisted off aboard a ship during a vicious storm. He was young then and the leg had quit growing.

As a child Darcy had watched Peter with fascination, and had in private tried to hop in his lively cricket style. She was convinced then that Peter knew how to do everything, and had never changed her mind about this.

The Strand, the broad handsome shopping area that stretched along the island parallel to Galveston Bay, was crowded with shoppers. On foot and in handsome carriages, both brightly dressed tourists and local citizens crowded the thoroughfare. With the rest of the state as dry and hot as a baking oven, people came from everywhere to enjoy the cool breezes off the gulf. Darcy, watching young people pass, felt strangely out of place. The only other women filling baskets with tinned goods and fresh produce were married women. Even down on the pier, she was the only person under thirty peering into buckets of shrimp and selecting the fresh crabs Hildy had put on her list.

By the time she was through, Peter was carrying a groaning basket under each arm. Then Darcy saw Michael. She caught her breath and ducked her head, hoping her ruffled bonnet would conceal her identity from him. She breathed with relief when she didn't see him glance her way. She didn't recognize the rig he was driving, but it was a fancy phaeton, crisply painted and fitted with fancy leather trim. The horses were lively, their heads high, as stylish as the smiling girl in the seat beside Michael. Michael was smiling, too, which somehow made her furious. "I hate him," she whispered fiercely to herself, flushing to remember how eagerly she had responded to that same bewitching smile only the afternoon before.

And as if the day had not turned sour enough, Alex appeared. He was waiting by the buggy when she and Peter returned. "I thought I recognized old Jemmy here," he said, patting the gelding's neck.

She smiled stiffly and accepted his hand to step up into the buggy.

"You're angry with me," he said, his tone apologetic. "You have every reason to be, too. I'm sorry about yesterday. I lost my head."

His tone was so abject that Darcy grinned. "You came closer than you know to losing your head," she admitted. "I almost bit it off."

When he smiled, she remembered why they had been friends for so long. He even looked different when his mother wasn't around. His dark eyes sparkled and that wonderful dimple creased his left cheek. "Could I apologize with a sarsaparilla? Maybe a dish of that chocolate ice cream you favor?"

"I'd love to," she admitted, then nodded toward the loaded buggy. "But Peter and I have to get all this stuff back home."

Alex peered into the buggy and laughed. "Hildy expecting another hurricane?" he asked.

Darcy nodded. It was a standing joke that even a stiff breeze was enough to make Hildy lay in extra supplies. "She and Papa both," Darcy told him. "Thanks again for the invitation. See you tomorrow night?"

"I'm counting the hours," he said. He touched her gloved hand briefly before he stepped back.

Darcy didn't realize Peter had been listening to their conversation until he turned the corner of C Street at 23rd. "Your pa and Hildy could be right," he called back to her. "Look at them flags."

Shielding her eyes with her hand, she stared up at the top of the Levy Building, where the weather bureau posted the weather flags. Indeed, a storm flag whipped from the pole.

"And the barometer is still dropping," Peter added dourly.

Darcy stared at the back of his head. Galveston had to be the only place in the world where every person in town knew how to read a barometer! As Jemmy clipped on toward home under an almost cloudless sky, Darcy mused that perhaps a flat, muggy Houston thirty miles from the gulf wouldn't be the worst place in the world to live after all.

Chapter Four

Friday, September 7, 1900

FRIDAY morning came hot, promising to fulfill the worst of Darcy's fears about her party. She even hated getting dressed. She thought wistfully of the "good old days" when she could let her hair hang loose and wear flat-heeled slippers. By the time she twisted her heavy dark hair up and fastened it with combs and clips, damp little curls began to spring free to paste themselves against her forehead.

Darcy's father had already left for the harbor when she came downstairs.

"He's fretting about the weather," Hildy explained as she brought in breakfast for Darcy and Rose. "The steamer *Pensacola* was scheduled to leave this morning about seven o'clock. Your papa couldn't believe Captain Simmons would keep his sailing date, not with the storm warnings out."

Darcy said nothing. She was sick and tired of even hearing about this stupid storm. She could use up all her fingers listing storms that had been tracked just as this one was. The wind had swung most of them away. Some had even blown away at sea and never struck land anywhere. This one had just better stay away from Galveston until her party was over!

Making lists of the work that needed to be done every day was a habit Hildy had picked up from Darcy's mother. With breakfast over, Darcy followed Hildy into the kitchen to see what last minute jobs Hildy had written on her "Friday" list.

Most of the notations were predictable:

Set buffet table
Fresh flowers for the tables
Chill plates for melons
Use rose mold for butter

The fifth item on the list was a question, heavily underlined:

Dance Programs?

Darcy shrieked. "Dance programs!" she cried, turning to Hildy. "I never for one moment even thought about dance programs."

Hildy smiled without taking her hands from the dough she was kneading. "Neither did I," she admitted. "That is, until I woke up at dawn in a cold sweat about them."

"But what can we do? We can't have a dance without programs. It's unheard of. And how would you know who to dance with next?"

"Now don't fly off panicky. I've thought of nothing else all morning. At first I thought maybe we could excuse ourselves because of the late change of plans," Hildy's tone was thoughful. "Then I had another idea — not the best maybe, but an idea."

Darcy was all but leaping up and down with impatience. "Tell me, Hildy," she pleaded. "Printing? Could we possibly have them printed?"

"Not a chance," Hildy said, shaking her head. "But nice linen paper is quickly bought and some bright cotton ribbon."

"But the dance order has to be written out, with numbers," Darcy protested.

"You write a clear, pretty hand," Hildy reminded her. "And you might even paint on a daisy to match the ribbon."

Darcy stared at her only a moment before running to hug her hard around her ample waist. "The gentlemen don't need programs," she decided. "I'll only have to make sixteen. Angela will help. I know she will."

"Rose is going to want to help," Hildy warned. "Maybe she could tie the ribbons."

When Darcy hesitated, Hildy glanced toward the door, then whispered quietly. "She doesn't have to make a bow, but just a loop to fit over the wrist. It would save hurting her feelings."

As Darcy dressed to go out, she wished, for the hundredth time, that her father would have a telephone installed. She didn't really blame him for not wanting to add that great expense for something so newfangled. Like the few gasoline buggies that coughed and clattered up and down the shell streets, her father had some doubt that such complicated toys would really last. But what a luxury it would be to be able to call Angela instead of having to go past her house!

Rose was at the piano filling the house with music when Darcy came back down. She paused and look doubtfully at Darcy. "Uncle asked me if I would play a few numbers for the party tonight. Will that embarrass you?"

"Not for a minute! I'm delighted."

"Uncle Amos said the pianist was good on the regular things but he especially wanted you to have some of the newer dances."

"The cakewalk?" Darcy asked, suddenly excited. The cakewalk was the most popular dance everywhere and Mr. Larkin, who was playing for the party, hadn't mastered the rhythm yet. (Angela said the closest he could come was a cookie crawl.)

"Like this?" Rose asked. As she spoke, she brought her hands down with a crash and set the piano to dancing in a rollicking cakewalk rhythm.

"You're wonderful!" Darcy cried, keeping the beat as she danced out the door.

Wonder of wonders, Angela was still at home. Not only that, but she was delighted to change her plans for such an unusual project.

"I wish I had known you girls were going to shop," Angela's mother told Darcy. "I have a silly list of things I need for Sunday."

"We'll be happy to get them for you," Darcy said.

Mrs. Morton smiled and touched her arm. "They aren't that important. I'm going to meet one of my friends. We'll start early tomorrow so we can both be back home by the time it gets hot." She took Darcy's face between her hands and smiled at her tenderly. "Happy sixteenth birthday, Darcy. And many, many more happy birthdays to come."

Darcy clung to her, feeling almost too emotional to thank her for her good wishes.

Again the Strand was crowded with shoppers. Everywhere they went, Darcy and Angela had to wait before being served. They finally found a paper stock that was just right, a heavy cream paper board with a nice texture to take watercolor. Angela was as excited as Darcy was. "Everyone will treasure them forever," she told Darcy.

After buying Wedgewood-blue cotton ribbon and a pan of matching watercolor, they started toward home. As they left the Strand, Darcy winced at the memory of seeing Michael there with that fancy-dressed girl the day before. Without meaning to, she found herself mentioning it to Angela. "I saw your cousin yesterday when I was out shopping," she said in a deliberately casual tone.

"So he told me," Angela replied. "He saw you but hoped you hadn't seen him."

Darcy stared at her. That had been her own reaction exactly. "He *appeared* to be having a good time," Darcy said primly.

"Oh, his manners are good enough when they *have* to be," Angela said with a shrug. "Yesterday they had to be. My father asked poor Michael to show the city to a visiting banker's daughter from Houston. Apparently she did nothing but chatter about money and bat her eyes at him. He was so glad to be shut of her I thought he was going to turn handstands in the foyer when he got back home."

Darcy giggled, feeling suddenly light-headed in spite of the heat. For a moment or two she seemed to be walking on air. Then Angela stopped so suddenly that Darcy almost ran over her. Angela was leaning way back, squinting upwards into the blazing summer sky.

"What are you staring at?" Darcy asked.

"That flag," Angela said. "I don't remember ever seeing one just like that before. You're better at this than I am; what do those flags mean?"

Darcy studied the flags fluttering wildly on the top of the Levy Building. How could she help knowing the weather flags when her father talked of little else? "The red flag with the black center means a violent storm is coming," she said thoughtfully, wondering if her father was going to be right after all. "The white pennant under it means the wind will come from the northeast."

Angela's eyes widened. "Does that mean a hurricane?"

"It's probably too early to tell," Darcy admitted. Then remembering how Angela's mother reacted to storms, she added, "If you want to go home to your mother, I'll understand."

Angela frowned a moment, then shook her head. "She knows our plans. If I went home, she'd guess right away that something was going on," she decided. "But let's hurry with the dance programs in case it gets worse."

Hildy's idea was a winner. Darcy privately thought the handmade programs were far more elegant than printed ones. Instead of daisies, she brushed a single blue pansy face on the fold of each program between the "order of dances." Rose bit her lips with concentration as she looped the blue cords in and tied them. The minute they were finished, Angela rose to go home.

"Has your father ever thought of taking your mother over to the mainland when a storm is coming?" Darcy asked. "It seems awful for her to go through this terror every time."

Angela wiped her moist face with her handkerchief and shook her head. "Mama's 'old Galveston,' " she reminded Darcy. "You know the pride these people take in never running from storms."

"Isn't that just a mite silly?" Rose asked in a hesitant voice.

Angela laughed and stroked Rose's streaming hair out of her face. "I'd say it was giant, huge, mammoth silly if they asked me. But needless to say, nobody ever has!"

Her birthday was the hottest day that Darcy could ever remember. Hildy insisted that Darcy take a nap late in the afternoon. She never really slept at all, but only twisted restlessly in the heat until she could finally get up to bathe and dress. Usually the late afternoon brought some relief. A brisk wind did rise, but it blew as hot as the breath of a blazing fire.

As Darcy dressed for her party, she drifted now and then to the window to look at the gulf. No matter how hot the house got during the party, her father had clearly made the right decision. Huge waves thundered onto the beach. And they looked different, ugly and dark and forbidding from the sand they carried.

At sunset the beach was usually crowded with late swimmers who avoided the brutal sun of mid-day. Today no swimmers braved those great dark waves, and only a few watchers were scattered along the beach. Even those hardy souls stayed well back from the ragged line of debris being cast on the beach by the giant swells.

In contrast to the violent turbulence of the sea, the sky was sketched with fragile brush strokes of pale clouds to the southeast. They seemed deceptively delicate, reflecting the fragile floral tints of the sunset. Darcy let herself be encouraged by this.

Her father had often talked of the "brick-dust" appearance of the sky when a hurricane was coming.

As she watched, the first rim of the moon broke the horizon and began its patient passage across the sky. It rose slowly, pale and immense against the blue, almost a full moon with its right side only nibbled away a little bit. On still nights the moon silvered a path across the water. The turbulence of this sea shattered the reflection into silver confetti rising and falling with the swells.

Partly because she had chosen blue cords on the dance programs and partly because it was made of sheer cotton that let the air in, Darcy chose the pale blue dress her Aunt Julie had sent for her birthday. Trimmed with deep ruffled flounces that fell to the hem, the dress would be perfect to dance in.

The moment Darcy saw her reflection in the mirror, she covered her bare throat with both hands. The low neckline showed an astonishing amount of her neck. She couldn't possibly be comfortable with her whole throat exposed. Yet she knew the dress was the very latest style. Then she realized what was wrong. In the magazines, such necklines were always shown with jewelry.

Darcy stared at herself. She had two kinds of jewelry. The padded chest covered with lacquered shells held the trinkets she had collected over the years. She went through the chest carefully. The heart-shaped locket had been a gift from Hildy. The strands of colored beads, none of them real, had come as birthday presents from playmates. There were bracelets of shells and a tiny ring she had worn as a baby.

Finally when nothing else worked, Darcy knelt and pulled up the secret panel hidden in the floor of her closet. She trembled as she set out the box of her mother's jewelry that her father had told her would be hers. Would she dare wear any of it? She had a right to, and this was certainly an appropriate day.

She had forgotten how beautiful her mother's things were: gleaming gold chains, a sapphire pendant surrounded by tiny seed pearls. The single strand of small pearls was the best.

The minute she held them up, she knew they were right. Holding the clasp behind her neck, Darcy twirled before her mirror. Maybe it wasn't all that bad to be grown up enough to wear elegant clothes. Sixteen. What a magical number that was. If she squinted her eyes just a little bit she could forget that she was only a girl with a heart-shaped face and a mass of coal-black curls. She was a graceful, stylish model from a picture in *Godey's Lady's Book*. She smiled at herself from behind an ivory fan and thought of Michael Stephens. With really good luck he would squint, too, and see her the way she saw herself!

Through her open window came the sound of horses' hooves and the trill of a woman's laughter. She folded the fan, leaned toward the mirror and slapped both her cheeks fiercely to bring up the color. As she glanced at her reflection, her eyes widened with horror, thinking of her father's reaction to the familiar jewels. She took off the pearls, thrust them in the shell box, and put on Hildy's locket. She was ready to greet her guests.

Chapter Five

Friday, September 7, 1900

ALEX came early, splendid in a single-breasted dress coat with silk reveres. He was as charming as he was handsome. Whatever else you could say about Mrs. Turner, she *did* know how to raise a gentleman. He knew all the guests and exactly how to greet them. He didn't exactly bow, but the angle of his body as he bent to lift a guest's hand in greeting clearly made every girl feel royal.

And when no guests were close, he turned playful and flattering. It was hard to remember why she had been so angry with him just two days before. In time, however, it got to be too much. Her guests would greet her, then drift away before she could talk to them. She got nervous about Michael's arrival. What would he think if he walked in and found

Alex lurking there, as if they were joined by an invisible chain?

And he *did* lurk, standing to her right and only a little behind as if he were an organ-grinder and she his pet monkey. When she moved across the room, he followed. She felt completely helpless and increasingly frustrated. *Now* she remembered why she had been so angry the day before, but what could she do? She couldn't exactly drive him away without creating a scene.

Her father, who was circulating among the guests, apparently saw both her rising annoyance and its cause. In any event, to her great relief, he joined them. After engaging Alex in small talk, her father drew him away to his study so she could greet her other guests without feeling self-conscious. More than anything, she wished for a chance to throw her arms around her father and hug him tight.

When a half hour had passed without any sign of Angela and Michael, Darcy felt a spinning spiral of concern rise in her chest. What could have happened to keep them away? She thought of the great sand-filled waves that had thundered on the shore as she was getting dressed. Had Angela's mother become so panicky from the possibility of a storm that they decided to stay with her? As time continued to pass, her concern turned to such a dull despair that she could hardly keep smiling at her guests.

For one thing, Darcy's dance program was filling up. It was only good manners for every male guest to ask the hostess to dance at least once. Alex had taken the first dance and the last before she caught her breath. A lot of the other names on her program were boys who had steady girls of their own. The thought of dancing with them when Michael hadn't even had a *chance* to ask for a dance was horrifying.

All the rooms were filled with chattering young people and Hildy and Peter were setting out dinner before Angela and Michael finally arrived. Not until they entered the foyer did Darcy realize how eagerly she had been watching for them. Angela, wearing pale sea-green, looked lovely except that her round face was flushed from the heat. Michael was as glowingly handsome as ever, and also as unpredictable. The moment he handed his hat and cane to Peter at the door he rose on tiptoe and openly scanned the room. When his eyes met Darcy's, he smiled with delight and began to make his way toward her in as near to a straight line as a man could possibly cut across a crowded room without actually knocking anyone down.

While Darcy was delighted by this, she felt herself flush a little. The other guests who had the misfortune to be in Michael's path stared first at him and then at her as they were thrust aside. And of course Alex saw the entire thing from the door of her father's study. To Darcy's horror, Alex started toward her in the same determined way.

Michael reached her first. "Darcy!" he said breathlessly. "If I haven't gotten here in time to get a birthday dance with you, I shall perish."

Darcy laughed. It was remarkable that she should feel so wonderfully bright and giddy after the way she had felt only moments before. "That would add a lot to my party, wouldn't it?"

"May I?" he asked, reaching for her dance program.

His pencil was ready. Before she could protest, he had written his initials in every remaining open dance.

"Michael," she cried, "what are you doing?"

"Only what I've planned since I heard about this party," he said, airily handing back the program. Then he frowned and pulled it over to look at it again. "Wait. Let me see that." After a moment's study, he looked up. "What's this AT on the first and last dance?"

"Alex Turner," Alex said coldly, from Darcy's other side.

"Oh, but that's not fair at all," Michael said. "You can have the first dance *or* the last dance but certainly not both of them. That wouldn't be sporting at all."

"Maybe sporting is not one of my ambitions," Alex said. "And who are you to tell me what dances I can have with my own girl?" Alex asked, his voice rising.

"Your own girl?" Michael asked dismissively. "I'd like to know what right you have to be so possessive!"

Darcy, conscious of the stares of her other guests, whispered fiercely, "Stop it, both of you. It's mine to decide with whom I dance."

When they only glared at each other, she threatened them, "If you don't stop that, I just plain won't dance with either of you."

Then, to her astonishment, she had the second chance in less than an hour to feel tender and grateful toward her father. He appeared before her, looking wonderfully distinguished and massive in his evening clothes. After a gallant bow, he offered his arm. "Please permit me the honor of escorting you to dinner," he said as formally as if they had only been introduced within the hour. When she glanced up at him and took his arm, he closed his other hand over hers and winked with a flash of his old merry mischief.

Her father's pace toward the dining room was slow and his voice so carefully modulated that no one but Darcy could possibly have caught his words.

"My dear Darcy, when you were only a rosebud in a ruffled bonnet, your mother warned me about this day. She was right, of course. If I must get used to fighting off ardent swains from my Darcy, I might as well start tonight."

She barely swallowed the giggle that rose in her throat.

Hildy had outdone herself. Darcy smiled at her father as they heard the guests' delighted comments about the beauty of the table and the marvelously garnished food. She felt as if she were in a kind of a dream. She might have thought this really *was* a dream if a small, winding stream of sweat had not steadily tickled its way down her back toward her corset.

With the meal over, Peter and another helper, who was brought in for the evening, cleared away the furniture and rolled up the rugs for the dance to begin. Like the Turners', many of the grander houses in Galveston had regular ballrooms, but Darcy's parents had decided against it. Darcy didn't mind at all not having a ballroom. Her parents were not the only ones who hesitated to give up an entire third floor to such an occasional use. Colonel Walter Gresham had spent a half million dollars on his handsome home on Broadway, and his dances were held on the main floor with the furniture moved back.

The moment the music began, both Alex and Michael faced her. Darcy's first impulse was to turn and flee. Instead, she felt a firm hand on her elbow. Her father's voice was rich as cream, with a warm smile behind it. "With your indulgence, gentlemen, I shall exercise my privilege as host and lead the guest of honor out for the first dance."

"Papa," Darcy whispered as he whirled her expertly in a waltz, "I love you."

"I saw you first," he reminded, winking in that wonderful raffish way again.

How could she have possibly thought that a beach party would be more fun than a dance? Indeed it was hot, so hot that the doors and windows had to be thrown open in spite of the brisk breeze. The pianist, Mr. Larson, did his usual fine job with all the favorite dance tunes. Not only that, but he yielded gracefully when Rose came to the bench for the first cakewalk, and clapped vigorously when she stumbled away from the piano in embarrassed pride.

At the intermission, Hildy and Peter refilled punch bowls one after the other, marching back and forth into the kitchen like toy soldiers. Darcy was giddy with pleasure. She knew for a certain fact that every single one of her guests was having a splendid time (with the possible exception of Alex Turner). The girls whose dance cards hadn't been filled even seemed to be having fun. Several of them joined the little groups that gathered around the piano to sing along with the music.

She should have guessed that Michael was an excellent dancer. When he led her in a whirling box waltz, Darcy felt herself as graceful as a seabird. During their second dance together, Alex tried to cut in, but Michael only whirled her away, giving Alex the choice of submitting gracefully or starting a scene. "My time is coming," Alex grumbled, walking away.

It was a glorious party, the party of every girl's dream. The only shadow was Alex, who stood dour and unsmiling, watching her dance with a glowering frown.

By popular demand, Rose came back to play another cakewalk for the next to the last dance. Michael's initials were on the card. The music had barely begun when Michael, his strong arm firm against her back, "walked" Darcy down the foyer, pushed open the front door and danced her out on the porch.

She gasped at the force of the wind. Ominous dark clouds had billowed in. They raced across the face of the shrunken moon, jostling and crowding each other in the dark, threatening sky. Seemingly unconscious of the whipping wind, Michael gripped her tightly, danced down the stairs, and into the shade of a giant palm tree. Positioning himself to protect her from the wind, he smiled down at her.

"Now," he said with satisfaction, "we can really talk."

It was anything but quiet out there. Between the rollicking music spilling out of the house and the thunder of the boiling surf, the air was filled with sound. But Michael stood very close so that his voice came firm and warm against her cheek.

"I have three things to tell you," he went on, shifting his body a little when the gusts of wind varied. "The first is that I have never seen you look more beautiful than you do tonight. And I have never seen you look less than beautiful. If that is rude, I'm sorry."

Darcy barely caught her breath before he went on. "I wanted to explain to you why I'm not staying here in Galveston. I haven't even told my uncle this yet.

"I want to stay, you know. More than you know

I want to stay — because of you. I know at times you have thought I was frightfully curious and abnormally interested in everything about this incredible place. It wasn't Galveston I cared about, Darcy, it was you. I burned to imagine everything about your life, what you liked, your experiences, what you knew, what you wanted from life. All of this because I wanted so much to be a part of your life.

"But without learning nearly enough about you, I learned too much about Galveston Island. Aside from you, this place is not what I'm looking for. I'm not even sure I could stand working with my uncle. Don't misunderstand me, he's a grand person and a wonderful human being. It's just that his business is not what I want. I'm an engineer, Darcy, not a builder. There's an immense difference. In a rich city like Galveston, a man can make a great living just building bigger houses, handsomer settings for other men's wealth. I need a place that needs my skill, where I can leave something more behind me than monuments to other men's pride. Does any of this make any sense to you?"

Darcy nodded. Some of it had made very confusing sense to her. He loved her and was leaving her.

"Try to understand," he begged. "Look at this little island, only thirty miles long and a couple of miles wide and it's already stiff with mansions of successful men. I want a challenge, Darcy. I *need* a challenge, something I can throw myself into with all the wit and energy I can muster. Surely you can understand that."

She only nodded because of the unexpected lump that had come into her throat at his words. Until this moment she hadn't realized how much she *wanted* him to stay. The past three weeks seemed suddenly so foolish and childish. She had fought against her feelings for him, been petty and critical of him to Angela. It had all been a lie and now he was going.

To her astonishment, he closed his arms around her and held her close. "There was a third thing, Darcy," he whispered. "I want to wish you the happiest birthday any beautiful young girl ever had. And a full, rich life to go with it."

As he spoke, he leaned and pressed his lips to hers. Feeling the warmth of his mouth on hers filled her with a most remarkable and totally unexpected delight. She didn't even realize she had put her arms about him until he finally pulled his lips away and pressed her head against his chest. "I may be rude, Darcy Dunlop. I may be rude and ungentlemanly, and a thorough cad for taking this advantage of you. But I'm honest, Darcy, and I love you with all my strength."

In that moment of near silence, she realized the music had stopped. She heard only the angry thunder of the waves and the rhythm of Michael's heart beating strongly against her.

A third sound was added to these, Alex's voice

calling. Michael held her close in the darkness and sighed. "Has his time really come?" he asked.

She wanted to cry "no" and cling to him, but again his arm was at her back as he led her from the shadow of the frantically bending palm tree toward the house. It was strangely light. In spite of the boiling sea, the sky was not as threatening as it had been only an hour before. The light of the moon was bright enough for Darcy to see Michael's face clearly. His expression was set, and as sad and wistful as she felt herself.

And Alex, with growing anger, continued to call "Darcy!" over the thundering tumult of the waves as she clung to Michael, sick at heart.

Chapter Six

Saturday, September 8, 1900

SLEEP was impossible. Long after the house was quiet, Darcy sat up straight in bed with her arms woven around her knees. Beyond her window in the boiling sky the moon seemed to be fighting for survival. Round and gleaming, it slid in and out among the towering black clouds as if it were pursued by the demons of the storm.

She turned, punched her pillow angrily and pulled up her covers. Why should she care what happened to that stupid moon? Dawn would come and the very next night the same moon would rise again, round and shining and carefree.

She wished she could say as much for herself. She tossed restlessly, trying to get comfortable. How could she be comfortable when she had found and lost love in the space of a couple of days? She was always teasing Angela about reading sentimental novels and being sloppy and romantic, but she had to be honest with herself.

Her relationship with Michael Stephens could have been lifted, chapter by chapter, from any one of a number of those books. She had resented hearing how irresistible he was, she had told herself he wasn't even attractive even as she thought about him all the time. Then, when she could no longer lie to herself about his appeal for her, he had kissed her in the shadow of a palm tree and the same as told her good-bye. What kind of romance novel would *that* make, with a miserable, unhappy ending?

"I think I hate him," she confided to her pillow, knowing that she wasn't being honest with herself again.

She slept, but only restlessly. The wind rose, rattling at her shutters and howling a little in the overhang of the eaves. Rose's whisper wakened her with a start.

"Darcy?" The younger girl's tone was timorous. "Could I just sleep in here with you? I'm scared."

"It's only a little wind," Darcy told her. The hands of Darcy's clock stood at four in the morning. Rose stood very still, not repeating her request but waiting for Darcy's decision with wide eyes. Her fair hair was tumbled and her usually smiling face was pinched with fear. She looked terribly vulnerable and childlike in her full-skirted, ruffled gown.

"Sure thing," Darcy said, relenting. She turned

back the covers on the far side of the bed and patted the sheet. "Hop right in, but no talking!"

Rose didn't talk but snuggled down at once. Within what seemed only minutes she was sleeping deeply and peacefully. Darcy envied her. The wind *was* so scary and loud against the wooden storm shutters that Darcy never lost consciousness of it.

This was great, she thought bitterly. Now she wouldn't even be able to go to the beach with her friends in the morning, either. At this rate she had completely wasted the money she spent on that wonderful bathing costume!

When the light of dawn shone through her shutters, a pattering of rain began against her windows. Darcy sighed, gave up, and crawled out of bed carefully so as not to disturb her cousin.

She groped in the closet for the wonderful birthday present her father had ordered sent in from one of the big stores in Dallas. She felt very sophisticated as she tied the satin strings tightly around her waist. The kimono was a rich flag-blue with marvelous satin flowers embroidered down the back. She wanted to see her father, to thank him for the really glorious party, and for being so thoughtful of her (although she didn't know how she could mention *that* without sounding conceited about her being attractive to men).

Halfway down the stairs, she frowned. The air was rich with the unmistakable fragrance of soda biscuits and bacon mingled with the sharp scent of coffee. Her father couldn't be up already! She ran down the rest of the stairs and straight to the kitchen.

Hildy looked over as Darcy swung the door open.

"Your papa?" She shook her head. "You missed him. He's dressed and gone already. I had to nail his coattails to the floor to get him to wait for breakfast. Then he ate it in here standing up and left without a second cup of coffee."

"I'm sorry I missed him," Darcy told her. "I wanted to thank him for last night."

"I can't believe you're up so early after such a grand festivity."

"It *was* a grand festivity," Darcy told her. "Your ears must have rung all evening from the way people bragged about the food. It looked beautiful and tasted the same. I don't know how you got it all done so splendidly."

Hildy smiled, her face reddening with pleasure. Then she tightened her lips. "It just about had to be special after what that Turner woman said to me."

Darcy shrugged. "Oh, pay no attention to her."

"I'm trying not to," Hildy grumbled, "but it isn't always easy."

Darcy perched on a wooden stool and yawned.

"See? You should pop back in bed and get some more sleep," Hildy said.

"Who could sleep?" Darcy asked. "The wind blew all night and now it's raining."

"I know," Hildy nodded. "That dog of yours got so upset that he barked himself hoarse."

"Where is he now?" Darcy asked, seeing that Buffy's rumpled basket in the kitchen corner was empty.

Hildy laughed. "Peter heard him clear out there in the carriage house and finally came in and got him. I'd guess they're bunked in out there together."

Darcy laughed. "Buffy wasn't the only one who got spooked. If you look for Rose, she's in my bed. She came in stiff with fear from the wind howling."

"I don't think the captain shut an eye," Hildy said. "But he must be comforted now. The wind was switching to the north when he left."

"Doesn't that mean that we'll have low tide?" Darcy asked, splitting a still-warm biscuit and setting a pat of butter inside it to melt.

"Your father's daughter," Hildy laughed. "He said exactly the same thing as he walked out that door."

Darcy went back upstairs at about eight. Rose was gone from her bed. The shutters still clattered from the wind. Darcy was all dressed and almost had her hair fastened up when she was startled to hear voices downstairs. Still groping with a horn pin that *would* pop out every time she had it in place, she went to the top of the stairwell to listen.

Michael's voice. And Angela's. She pulled the bedroom door shut, frowning. Angela was a slug in the morning. What in the world had ever gotten her out and about this early? She and Michael couldn't mean to go swimming with the rain still coming down. And it was too early anyway.

She ran down the stairs without waiting for Hildy to call. Michael, standing with his umbrella in the foyer, smiled up at her. "Look who else is up bright and early," he said. "We just came on the chance you might be. How does it feel to be sixteen plus a day?"

"Sleepy," she told him with a grin, then looked questioningly at Angela.

"I know you didn't expect us," Angela said swiftly, "but we were out and *had* to come by. You simply must come down and look at the beach. You've never seen anything like it!"

"You were out?" Darcy asked. "This early?"

Michael spoke up. "Angela's mother had some errands downtown. With the weather so uncertain, Uncle asked us to have her down there when the shops opened. That way she could get back home early if the weather worsened."

"How uncertain *is* the weather?" Darcy asked thoughtfully. Angela's father was almost as weather-conscious as her own. He certainly wouldn't agree to his wife going down to the Strand if he was really concerned.

"Papa's barometer was down to below 29.97 when he checked it this morning," Angela said. "But with the wind from the north, he felt it would be safe early."

"All right, all right," Michael said, spreading his hands in defeat. "You people have the strangest way of talking in English without making sense to a stranger. I've heard people talk about the barometer falling all week and I still haven't the vaguest idea what it means."

"If you mean to come live in Galveston, you'll learn soon enough," Angela laughed.

Darcy felt Michael's glance and dropped her eyes. If only he *were* planning to stay in Galveston. Her private knowledge that he was leaving made her breath come short. She spoke swiftly into the sudden awkward silence.

"Barometers measure air pressure," she said, still a little shocked by the low reading Angela had reported. "It falls when a storm is coming and rises for good weather. How are you going to know when to pick your mother up?"

Angela shook her head. "We don't have to do that. She's meeting a friend who'll get her home," Angela said. "Come on, get your rain clothes. The beach is a free show!"

Hildy frowned her disapproval from the end of the hall. "The wind sounds fierce out there," she warned.

"We won't stay long," Michael assured her. "Where's Rose?"

"Still tucked in bed, I hope," Hildy said. Her tone turned stern. "I don't suppose it will hurt. But you will watch out for our girl, hear me?"

"With my life," Michael promised earnestly with

a sly grin at Darcy. Unaccountably her heart jumped at his words.

They weren't the only people heading for the beach. A street car passed and then another, both loaded with passengers wearing oilskins and carrying umbrellas.

"If there's going to be a crowd, we'd be better off without the buggy," Angela suggested.

"You're probably right," Michael agreed. He gave the horse a pat as they passed the hitching post and set off.

The rain had slackened off to a steady, cool drizzle, which dimpled the surfaces of the puddles that stood in the low places along the sides of the streets. There was plenty to watch in their brief walk toward the gulf. Within the block, a panicked runaway horse charged up the street. Michael lunged for his reins but missed. The animal swung around the corner, turned into a gate, and clattered up the front stairs into a house.

"I hope those people are expecting company," Darcy said, giggling. The wind was at their backs. Small boys squatted to sail their toy boats in the streams of water moving along the edges of the street.

Before they reached the beach they passed a couple of small, two-wheeled bathhouses which had been blown in by the gale. These had been dumped on the street, upside down and on their sides.

"Maybe I'd better hang on to you two," Michael said, gripping Darcy and Angela by the arms. "It would be pretty undignified to have you blown off your wheels like that."

Crowds of people, many in rain gear and waterproof hats, were gathered all along the beach. Some brave cyclists waggled their bicycles along the hard sand and a number of small buggies and rigs were parked where their passengers could stare up at the drama in the sky. The sea was a boiling darkness under the looming dark clouds on the horizon. White-capped swells rolled inexorably toward the watchers. Darcy marveled to herself that the tide could be running so high with the wind driving against it from the north.

Darcy felt strange, as if she were suspended somewhere, restless and waiting. Was this because of her increasing concern about the storm, or because of her confused feelings about Michael? She was vibrantly conscious of the warmth of his hand on her arm and ashamed of the feeling it gave her. Was she going to feel this way for a whole week until he left? She couldn't stand it, she really couldn't.

They had only gone a few blocks west along the beach before Angela spied an immense conch shell, half buried in sand a few yards ahead. She ran across the ring of flotsam to grab it before a wave came in to retrieve it.

The instant she left them, Michael turned urgently to Darcy. "You aren't angry with me?"

When she shook her head, he gripped her arm more tightly. "I didn't do a lot of sleeping last night," he admitted. "I had no right to steal you off that way, nor to kiss you the way I did."

Darcy didn't look up at his words.

"But you're not angry?" he asked again.

When she only shook her head again, his tone turned to exasperation.

"Don't just waggle your head at me like that, Darcy. Say something! Don't you realize how much your feelings matter to me? I didn't plan to do that, it just came over me. You're the only one I've talked to about either my plans or how I feel about you."

"I'm not angry, Michael," she told him.

"Thank goodness," he said, tightening his grip on her arm. "Darcy, this is the toughest thing I've ever done in my life and I'm having trouble dealing with it. Falling in love was *absolutely* the last thing I thought of when I came down here. Now just thinking about having to leave you is horrible. Besides that, I've probably messed you up with Mr. Scowly, too," he added.

She smiled in spite of herself. "The name is Turner."

"I hate him," Michael said sullenly.

"You're the one who's decided to leave," Darcy reminded him, breathless at her own boldness.

He stopped and stared at her. "What does that mean?"

Before she could catch her breath to answer, Angela came running. Her gait was awkward against the wind and she clutched the giant shell in both hands. "Look down the beach, Darcy," she gasped, winded from running. "What do you suppose is going on?"

They turned to see a man racing along the beach in a rough cart drawn by a single horse. He was lashing the beast as the cart careened along. He was shouting at the watchers as he went. The wind whipped his words from his lips so that Darcy could only hear his anguished tone. A lot of the crowd seemed to ignore him, but others were gathering their things and trailing back toward the town. A gang of young men and boys ran along beside the cart, trying to keep pace with his horse as they shouted and hooted at him.

"One if by land and two if by sea," Michael said.

Darcy stared at him.

"You know, Paul Revere with his lantern warning the colonists," Michael explained. "Only he doesn't have a lantern and the British aren't coming."

Darcy shaded her eyes to stare at the oncoming cart and its driver. "Cline," she cried suddenly. "That's Isaac Cline, the forecaster at the weather bureau. What's he doing out here?"

Michael stared at Darcy, then seized both her and Angela by their arms. "Weather bureau? Come on, let's go see what he's saying."

As the cart drew nearer, Mr. Cline's words became clear. "Go back to your homes," he shouted. "Seek shelter! A tropical cyclone is coming."

Darcy had never seen Mr. Cline look this way. He was not a very old man, probably still in his late thirties as her own father was. But he looked positively haggard, with dark shadows of fatigue under his eyes and his hair blown every which way by the wind. "Go home," he shouted, his voice hoarse from strain and edged with frustration.

Michael stood very still a moment. "Tropical cyclone," he repeated. "Is that the same as a hurricane?"

"It could be," Darcy said. "I've heard Papa say Mr. Cline never uses the word 'hurricane.' He's very much a scientist." For herself, her mind kept going back to her father. The wind was from the north. He was at the harbor, which was on the north side of the island. What was it like over there? Did they just have an overflow or was the bay whipping giant swells onto the piers? There were usually five or six ships down by the east end of the island with ten or twelve steamships moored along the wharf front, where her father would be.

Michael tightened his grip on the arms of both girls. "The warning of a scientist is good enough for me. Come on, let's go."

As they turned away from the gulf, one of the young men chasing after the cart turned and hooted at them. "You gonna listen to that crazy?" he asked with a sneer.

Michael shrugged and hastened Darcy and Angela along. Behind them many of the watchers stood impassively as if Mr. Cline's words were only the howling of the storm. When they reached the street where a crowd had gathered, they all turned for a last look at the boiling clouds and violent surf.

Alex broke from the group to appear suddenly at Darcy's side. She turned, startled by his acid voice. "This is a cozy little threesome," he said. "I almost didn't believe Hildy when she said you had actually come down here."

"You're here, aren't you?" Michael asked.

"I wasn't talking to *you*," Alex said. "Listen, Darcy. The barometer's still falling. Mother wants me to bring you and Hildy and Rose over to our place. Broadway's the highest point on the island, you know."

"That's very kind of you," Darcy said, conscious of Michael glowering at her side. He had tightened his grip on her arm so that it was almost painful. "But I don't think it's necessary. This is only an overflow so far."

"Over here, maybe," Alex said. "But the bay is moving steadily this way. The waves are already washing up over the railroad tracks to the mainland. What do you think sent Mr. Cline over here in such a state? The water is already knee-deep all along the north side."

As he spoke, the rain quickened, changing from a steady drizzle to a downpour. Darcy clutched her rain hat and glanced at Angela. "Listen, Alex.

Thank your mother for her offer. We'll be all right. We really will. Now we have to run or we'll drown standing up."

"Darcy," Alex said, his tone suddenly heavy with authority.

"I think you understood Miss Dunlop," Michael said, taking a step closer to Alex and looking him hard in the eyes.

Freed from Michael's grip, Angela seized Darcy's hand. "Come on, Darcy, let's go. I want to check on my mother."

Darcy went willingly, not at all eager to hear any more of this exchange between Alex and Michael. They had crossed a street and gone about a half block before Michael caught up. His expression was cold and his eyes flashing. Whatever had passed between the two of them had left Michael as angry as Alex had been.

The water had risen at least a foot since they had left. The street was a river with only the taller shrubs thrusting through the water concealing the lawns. Small waves lapped against the foundations of many of the houses.

"Have you ever seen it this bad before, Angela?" Michael asked his cousin.

"Never," she said.

He nodded briskly and began to plan out loud. "We'll drop you at home, Darcy, then take the buggy and check on your mother, Angela. Does this overflow ever get up into houses?"

"Only during really bad storms," Angela said.

"See, all the foundations are very high, with the first floors built above the tide level."

Hildy must have been watching from inside the door. The moment they neared the buggy, she came out on the porch.

"Is Rose with you?" she called.

Darcy and the others stared at each other. "No," Michael called. "Did she leave?"

Hildy, who was usually as calm as a sunny Sunday morning, twisted her apron between her hands. "About twenty minutes ago. Where could she have gone?"

Darcy felt a moment of panic. Where could Rose have gone? More to the point, where *would* she have gone?

"Didn't she say anything when she left?" Darcy asked.

Hildy shook her head. "Peter came in telling about the overflow west of here and she just shot out the door. She didn't even take a rain hat."

"West," Darcy echoed. "Saint Mary's Orphanage," she decided aloud. "That's the only place Rose ever goes except with me. Maybe she thought she could help the sisters with the children if the water was rising over there."

"Where is this orphanage?" Michael asked.

"A ways past our house," Angela told him.

"We'll look for her, Hildy," Michael called. "Jump in, you two."

The horse, skittish from standing ankle-deep in water, danced off sideways as they got into the buggy. Michael clucked him back. "We'll check at home and then look for Rose," he told Angela.

Darcy gripped her hands tightly in her lap, suddenly cold. All along the street their neighbors who lived in frail wooden houses were packing possessions down the front walks and putting them into buggies and onto wheeled carts. People she couldn't remember ever seeing before slogged along the flooded streets. The men moved with greater ease. The women had to fight to stay on their feet with the rising current tugging at their long full skirts, which were sodden and heavy with water. A young mother, holding a tiny infant against her shoulder and urging along a toddler in her wake, sloshed doggedly along the flooded street toward the higher ground near the middle of the island.

The buggy lurched and Darcy caught Angela's hand. It was ice-cold.

"You know your mother got home all right," Darcy whispered, trying to reassure her. Angela nodded, but her eyes looked unnaturally bright as if she was fighting back tears of terror.

Darcy felt a cold clutch in her own chest. Where was her father? Would he come home to her and Hildy or risk his own safety trying to save his schooner?

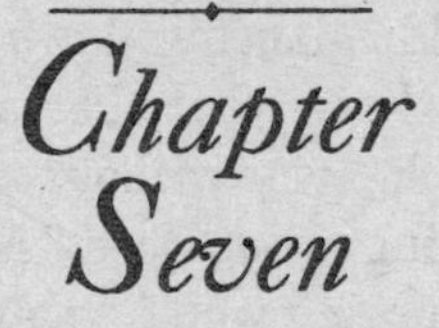

Chapter Seven

Saturday, September 8, 1900

GETTING to the Morton house proved to be more difficult than it had sounded. Michael tried one route after another in an effort to avoid forcing the nervous horse to wade through deep water. He drove in silence, concentrating on keeping the animal under control. Although Darcy and Angela didn't talk, the tension of Angela's rising concern was as eloquent as a shout. Only after making a series of detours that didn't work did Michael finally manage to turn into the block where his aunt's house stood. The street ran full of water, all the way onto the lawns. Water lapped at the stairway leading to the elevated front porch of the Morton house. With its wooden storm shutters shut tightly against the wind and rain, the house looked bleak and deserted.

Angela gathered her wet skirts in one hand and

leaped out of the buggy before Michael could rein the horse to a complete stop. Gripping her treasured shell high against her chest, she waded awkwardly toward the porch without even looking back.

"Should I go with her?" Darcy asked, uncertain what to do.

Michael shook his head. "You're already wet enough," he said, glancing down at her skirt and shoes. "Wait and see what she has to say."

Darcy sighed heavily without realizing it.

"You're thinking about Rose," Michael said, turning to her. "Worrying won't do any good. Anyway, Rose has a better chance than most girls in a crazy situation like this one."

She stared at him. "How can you say that?"

He grinned at her and shrugged. "Come on, Darcy. Think about it. That funny little cousin of yours is so used to having things go wrong that she takes disaster for granted. I've seen her pick herself up laughing from situations that would make an ordinary person curl up and quit."

Darcy couldn't argue with this.

"Which reminds me," he went on. "I meant to mention this before, but Rose was a shock to me. She's so very blonde and blue-eyed that I was startled when I met her. I guess I expected any first cousin of yours to have your dark, exotic coloring."

Darcy decided to ignore that strange word "exotic," which she was sure had never been applied to her before. "I take after my father," she explained. "But my mother's family is very fair."

"That must make it hard for your father sometimes," he said thoughtfully. "Angela says your mother was a perfectly wonderful person, and beautiful besides."

"She was all of that," Darcy agreed quietly. His words had set her mind into a whole new train of thought. Did Rose remind her father of his dead wife? Was part of his withdrawn reserve due to how different Darcy was from her fair, delicate mother?

Before she could really explore the question with her mind, the door of the Morton house swung open and Angela came out. She had removed her hat but shielded her hair with her hands as she came halfway down the stairs.

"Is Auntie there?" Michael called before she could speak.

Angela shook her head, her lips tight. "Papa's off getting her now," she told him. "He left instructions for me to wait here in case she beat him home." She nodded to the house behind her. "He rounded up a gang of helpers. They're in there rolling up rugs and moving furniture upstairs."

"You need my help?" Michael called.

Angela shook her head again and backed up one step to escape the rapidly rising water. "We'll be fine," she called. "Just take care of Darcy and find that silly Rose."

"You get out of those wet clothes or you'll be sick," Darcy called to her.

Angela made a face at her. "You sound like Hildy," she said. "And anyway, look who's talking!"

Michael hesitated, looking back at his cousin as if in doubt.

"Listen, Michael," Darcy said. "Don't fret about Rose and me. Your place is here with Angela and your family."

"I get to decide where my own place is," he told her with that wonderful smile. "Now, how do I get to this orphanage where Rose spends her time?"

"That way," Darcy said, pointing to the west. The horse, chilled and winded from dragging the sodden buggy along the flooded streets, fought the reins and danced nervously in the braces. Although Michael tried to drive in the direction she pointed, the flooded streets and an occasional fallen tree limb forced him to veer steadily more north than west.

Darcy gripped her hands in her lap, trying to control her rising panic. The wind had risen, whipping the water into a frenzy. This storm had to be almost over. Surely it would "spend itself" any minute. The wind *had* to drop. The west end of the island, being lower, was rapidly becoming a part of the gulf. The swells had lifted whole blocks of frail wooden houses from their foundations. These pitched and rolled in the tide that rose steadily as Darcy and Michael skirted its edge. In among the battered houses floated buggies, chicken coops filled with squawking poultry, and whole sides of houses torn loose to sail along among the uprooted trees.

"We won't ever get there going north this way," Darcy told him. "St. Mary's is very close to the beach."

He turned and looked at her. "Darcy, if it's close to the beach we can't get there at all." His voice was very level and quiet.

"But what about Rose?" she asked, fighting a new surge of rising panic.

"You don't *know* that Rose is there," Michael reminded her. "And surely they've evacuated the place by now. Look around you."

She didn't want to look around her. She'd already seen more destruction than she would ever be able to forget. Darcy covered her face with her hands for a moment, then swiftly pulled them away. She couldn't panic, she absolutely couldn't. "What do *you* think we should do?"

Michael hesitated, then took her hand. "I need to know some things. How safe is your house?"

"It's solid," she said. "We lost our house in the big fire when I was little, maybe about three. That was when the city had everyone put on slate roofs to keep fire from spreading again. Papa tried to build this one to get through storms. He built it of cypress, which doesn't warp from water. The walls are very thick and solid. We've had some bad storms since he built it and hardly any damage at all."

"Any hurricanes?"

She nodded. "The one when Angela's mother was hurt so badly."

"Then Hildy's safe," he decided aloud. "To be honest, Darcy, I don't think we could go back that way even if we wanted to. We need to move to higher ground."

"You don't want to go back to Angela's?"

"I'm staying with you."

She looked at him, at the thoughtfulness in his eyes and the firm set of his face. "What are you thinking?" she asked.

He looked at her. It wasn't much of a smile but he tried. "It's almost noon, Darcy. I'm thinking this has gone on a long time. I don't know anything about these storms but we've already fought this one for four hours, and the rain started earlier. All of a sudden I'm interested in barometer readings, too."

She smiled ruefully. "We'll make a Galvestonian of you yet." She instantly regretted her words. Would he think she was trying to make him stay? She went on swifly. "The weather bureau is in the Levy Building north of here, just a block or so from the Strand."

"Isn't that pretty close to the wharf area?" he asked. "Maybe you could check on your father at the same time."

She nodded, wanting to hug him for his thoughtfulness.

Even the horse's spirits seemed to lift as they started north. When they reached the high point of the island on Broadway, it was hard to believe the destruction they had left. The wind was strong with gusts that nearly tore the top off the buggy, but the streets were only flooded with rainwater, not littered with flood debris as they had been farther west and south. Those same streets, however, were crowded with whole families carrying bags and bundles.

"Where are they going?" Michael asked.

"To friends who have stronger houses," she explained. "Sometimes we've had fifty or more people come wait in our house until a storm passes."

There on Broadway Darcy thought with guilt of Alex and his mother. Mrs. Turner *had* been thoughtful to send Alex for her, only to have him caught in an ugly confrontation with Michael.

As they moved on north, the conditions became steadily worse again. The wharf area was under siege, with mammoth waves thundering against the anchored craft and surging onto the buildings along the piers, many of which had collapsed under the spray. Her father's schooner, *Sojourner*, tossed like the others, but seeing it still moored there comforted Darcy. She stood with Michael a long time, hoping to catch a glimpse of her father or his crew, but no one ventured above deck.

"Feel better?" Michael asked, his hand at her back to brace her against the wind.

"A little," she admitted. "He has all the lines out. It should weather the rest of this. They're safer in that cabin than almost any place they could be."

"Then come on," he said, taking her arm firmly.

The downtown area was like another world. Although high water coursed along the streets, it looked like an ordinary flow, the natural result of a morning or sporadic heavy rain. Many of the businesses were closed, which was unusual for a Saturday, but some merchants served their trade or watched the rising flood from their doorways.

Darcy unconsciously watched for Angela's mother and father among the pedestrians crowding the streets. One of Galveston's few gasoline buggies had apparently encountered more water than it could handle. It had been abandoned, forcing the horse-drawn carriages to make wide detours around it.

The calm of the street ended abruptly as the wind rose. Suddenly the level of noise became incredible. This gale, carrying every kind of debris, smashed the windows of the upper stories of buildings, spraying the street with shards of broken glass. Women screamed and horses reared and whinnied in terror.

Michael pulled the buggy to the side of the street and pulled on the brake. "What are you doing?" Darcy asked as he leaped out and fastened the horse loosely to a hitching post.

"Using my head for a change," Michael said, looking up at her with that brilliant smile. He offered her his hand to step down from the buggy. "We passed an open restaurant back there. I'm going to get you in out of this flying glass and we'll have something to eat."

"I don't believe you," she cried. "You want to stop to eat at a time like this?"

"At a time like this you eat when you can," he told her.

"But what about the weather prediction?" she asked.

"I'll call them on the telephone until I get somebody to answer me. See, I really *am* using my head! And, Darcy, this can't last much longer. It has to blow itself out soon!"

Darcy hadn't been hungry until the rich smells of the Elite Restaurant kitchen met her at the door. There were few open tables in the room, but Michael insisted that they wait for one against the back wall near the kitchen. "There are tables by the window," Darcy pointed out.

"I didn't bring you in here to be hit by a broken plate window," he told her.

The waiter brought them fragrant, steaming coffee with the menus. After barely tasting his coffee, Michael went to the phone to make his first unsuccessful attempt to get the weather bureau. After they ordered their meals, he called again, and was back at the telephone when their meals were served. She lost track of how many times he left to use the telephone, only to be unable to get through to the weather bureau a single time.

"I feel like a jack-in-the-box," he said, slipping back into his seat. Then he looked over at her and laughed. "This is wild. Ever since I first met you, I've been hoping to get some time alone with you. So how do I get it? With both of us dripping wet and half-starved and the city swimming in its own juices."

"What an awful way to put it!" Darcy protested. Then she laughed softly, too. "If it makes you feel any better, I've never spent this much time with any young man in my lengthy sixteen years."

"Not even Mr. Scowly?"

"His name is Turner," she said loyally. "Of course not. Alex and I behave very properly. I don't know the rules for young people where you come from, but here a gentleman only calls by appointment and it's only proper to stay twenty minutes to a half hour. Is it different in New England?"

"I wouldn't really know," he said airily. "I've never *wanted* to stay with any girl longer than that before." He leaned toward her with a look of mischief. "Does that rule still hold after you're engaged?"

"Well, no," Darcy admitted.

"Fine," he said, sitting up happily. "Just agree to marry me when you're all the way grown up and we can spend all our time together until I leave."

Darcy caught her breath with shock, and then laughed. "You are mad, absolutely mad!"

"This from a lady who lives on a little sandbar out in the middle of a vicious sea?" he asked.

She blinked at this rude description of the city she loved. "Is that really how you see Galveston?"

He nodded soberly. "It really is," he admitted. "But you have to remember I'm an engineer. This whole place has to be a kind of unique insanity. With its beaches and flowers and trees and gentle people, it is like an earthy paradise poised at the gates of destruction. And the worst of it is that it doesn't have to be like that. This island could be made reasonably safe for human habitation."

"By a seawall, I guess." Now he was really beginning to sound like her father, who had talked "seawall" as long as she could remember.

He nodded. "It's been done other places. But Galveston needs more than that. The island itself needs to be brought up higher above the sea level."

"So I guess you want to lift up an entire city and stick dirt under it?" she asked caustically. "Now who's mad?"

"I was thinking about sand rather than dirt," he admitted. "They must dredge that ship channel to keep it open. And there's nothing under that gulf but sand. And don't laugh! Chicago did something like that several years ago when that city was sinking below the level of Lake Michigan."

"But this island is covered with big buildings, not just lakeside shanties," she reminded him. Angela was always accusing *her* of exaggeration. She wasn't in a class with Michael.

He leaned toward her, his eyes intense. "Lakeside shanties nothing! Pullman, the railroad man, and some other contractors raised an entire city block at the same time."

Darcy looked down at her plate. "Of course they did, Michael. With mirrors."

"You are unbelievable," he said, his tone as cross as she'd ever heard it. "He used jackscrews, six thousand of them, with six hundred men turning them together just a fraction of an inch at a time. As the buildings rose, they were shored up with timbers. The block was raised four feet in that many days and business went on all the time. They didn't even spill any of the wine on the hotel dining tables."

She shook her head. "I give up. That's too wild a story for you to have made up." As she spoke, she heard the crashing of more windows breaking and the screams of people in the street outside. She touched Michael's hand. "I'm glad you chose this table. You even made me forget the storm for a few minutes."

"Then you *will* be engaged to me?" he asked in mock eagerness.

"Oh, go make your telephone call," she laughed.

Darcy amazed herself by eating an immense amount of food, finishing all of her chowder, then cleaning up a heaping plate of spiced shrimp with rice.

"Good girl!" Michael said. "Food could be a problem with all these homeless people and drowned kitchens."

"I expect a lot of families have a Hildy to take care of that. Every time the wind rises, she lays in fresh tinned goods. She has enough food stored in our attic to feed the army over at Fort Crockett."

Michael's call finally got through to the weather bureau. He was gone a long while and came back frowning. "The wind gauge has blown away," he told her. "The barometer is at 29.166 and still falling."

"Michael," Darcy gasped.

"That doesn't sound like much change," he said.

"I have never in my life heard of a reading that low," she told him.

"The last thing the man said was to seek shelter on high ground," Michael added. Darcy's mind went to her father's ship, frantically straining against its moorings in the bay.

Michael had placed her in a chair facing the wall. She hadn't thought anything about it at the time. Now she started to turn around to look toward the street. Michael took her hand and shook his head urgently. "Don't look, Darcy. Please don't look. We need to talk first."

She stared at him, startled at his tone. He didn't release her hand but gripped it firmly and leaned toward her.

"Now listen to me without talking for a minute. It's gotten a lot worse out there very fast. Only the raised foundation has kept the water out of this room. There's death out there, flying death with the debris, the bricks, those murderous flying slates. You can *see* the water rise."

When she started to speak, he gripped her hand harder. "No," he said. "Let me finish. It's only going to be a matter of minutes before this place is flooded, too. I'm going to take you somewhere you can be safe. You have to help me get you to the Turner house."

"No!" she cried.

"Yes," he said swiftly. "Please don't argue with

me. You *have* to be safe. The Turners live on Broadway, don't they? You said Broadway was the highest point. How many stories in the Turner house?"

"Three," she stammered. "But, Michael, please. I don't want to go there. Let me stay with you."

He shook his head. "The only thing that matters is keeping you safe," he insisted.

"It is *not*," she said fiercely. "What about my family? Papa? Hildy? Rose?"

He sighed heavily. "Listen to me," he said quietly. "Every time I've gone out for that phone I've had to wait in line and hear what the people are saying, Darcy. This isn't anything like the storms you remember; it's a hundred times worse. The water is already three feet above the wharf on the bay side. The west end of the island is swept clean. On the east side nothing is left standing in the first twelve blocks in from the gulf. The police have abandoned their patrol buggies and are evacuating people by boat. I intend to try to get you to the Turner house. Lacking that, I'll find you other shelter."

She fought a sudden rising panic. Did she have to believe Michael? Rumors always raged during a time of crisis. Was he overstating the conditions because he was a stranger? How could he expect her to forget about her own family? She took a deep breath and put her head back for a moment. Her hands hurt from his grip. When she opened her eyes to look at him, his eyes were stern on hers.

"Don't try to fight me on this, Darcy," he said,

his tone threatening. "Because I'm not going to let you get away with it."

She never knew what else he meant to say. At that moment a flying brick hit the plate glass window that looked out on the street. The storm swept in, carrying water and broken glass and tumbling pieces of lumber. The other diners screamed and leaped to their feet, knocking over chairs and tipping tables. The wind and water swept the linen and dishes from the tables, filling the air with flying food and cutlery.

Michael was on his feet at once, sheltering her with his body. She clung to him, unable to believe the chaos around them. "Hang on to me, Darcy," he shouted. "We're going to make a run for shelter. Now."

Chapter Eight

Saturday, September 8, 1900, 2:30 p.m.

As Darcy passed through the doorway of the Elite Restaurant, the wind-driven rain struck her like the blow of a fist. As she staggered back, gasping at the shock of its force, the crowd behind her shoved her down the stairs. She fought to keep from being driven to her knees. The rain pounded at her exposed face with the force of hail, flooding her with waves of sudden pain. Only Michael's firm grip kept her from being swept into the writhing torrent that raced along the street. The water was waist-deep, a swirling nightmare of fleeing people, floating debris and horses whose frantic neighing failed to drown out the howling of the wind and the screams of terrified people.

Darcy clung to Michael, shutting her eyes against

the pandemonium around her. The crowd seemed to be fighting its way toward the Tremont Hotel only a few blocks away. The crush of people bore them along in spite of the leaden weight of Darcy's saturated clothing.

Only Michael's steady grip and constant words of encouragement kept Darcy moving that next half hour. Horror pressed itself in vivid scenes against her anguished eyes. Just ahead of Darcy, an elderly woman wearing a feather-trimmed hat lost her footing and disappeared under the brackish, whirling waves, not to emerge again. A man carrying an unconscious child pushed past Darcy, weeping as he clung to his small burden. The sky was dark with flying debris and the howling and whistling of the wind vibrated through Darcy's skull.

Just when she thought that her mind had accepted the ultimate horror she could bear, a roof slate as sharp as the blade of Hildy's cleaver spun from the looming darkness to strike the man struggling at Darcy's side. One moment she saw his face, haggard with exhaustion and panic. The next moment it was gone. The slate had sliced his head neatly from his body. His head bobbed beside her a moment before sinking. His body slid beneath the water as if gripped by an invisible hand.

She began to scream. "No!" she protested. "No, no, no!" Her voice was lost among the cries of those around her and the remorseless howling of the wind.

They were within a few steps of the front of the

Tremont Hotel when the storm wave came. Four feet of solid water rolled in toward them, its top surface as smooth as a sheet of ebony glass. It was a mountain of water, curled and dark and grasping. Gasping and flailing, Darcy fought to rise through it to the dark air above. The water that forced itself into her face and down her throat made her suddenly ill.

She coughed and emptied her mouth only to realize that the taste remaining was sea salt.

Her last hope died. This was gulf water. The rising gulf had completely covered the island to meet the fresh water flood coming in from the bay. Galveston was all the way under water. She went limp in Michael's grip. It was over. In the swirling dance of the joined waters, she felt herself spinning helplessly and didn't even care. The water that had been waist-deep now was over the heads of the tallest men. The only people riding the crest of that wave were swimmers like herself and Michael. The screams of the drowning stopped suddenly as the current tugged them under.

Michael was dragging her, his voice rough and urgent between his teeth. "Swim, Darcy, swim," he ordered, his grip painful on her arms. A wave caught them, sweeping them around the corner. Darcy felt her head snap with a jerk as she suddenly stopped. "Hold on to me, Darcy," Michael shouted. "Help me."

It took her a moment to realize that Michael had

been thrown against a high iron fence. She groped for the slender metal upright and wove her arms around it. By wrapping her legs around the rods of the fence she could tighten her body almost flat against it to resist the pull of the raging water.

Michael pressed her painfully against the biting iron and pleaded with her. "The water is still rising. When it crests this fence, we are in trouble again. Help me, Darcy. You know the city. Where can we try to get to?"

She shook her head.

His tone was suddenly angry. "Big buildings, Darcy. Buildings too strong to be carried away. Think!"

She wanted to tell him that the huge hotel they had just been swept past was their best chance. That was no good. She had to think of new hopes. Her mind split between the problem he pressed on her and the terror of seeing entire houses spin past them in the torrent. She couldn't think. She couldn't look. She couldn't keep from seeing. Worst of all, she couldn't shut out the cries of pain and terror rising all around them.

Michael shook her. "Think!" he ordered. "Our lives depend on you."

"Rosenberg School," she gasped. "St. Mary's Infirmary, City Hall."

Why didn't he let her alone? Nothing was going to save them. He had been right. Galveston was only a sandbar, and the gulf had reclaimed its own.

As the water continued to climb, Michael forced her to fight her way upward with him. Then they were at the top, where the fence ended in sharp finials. A surge of water swept toward them, carrying a large wooden door.

"Hang on," Michael yelled at her but his words meant nothing. The fence disappeared beneath her. She flailed desperately, swept along in a tide of struggling animals, lumber, and corpses tumbling over and over in a ludicrous imitation of life.

"Your hand, Darcy," Michael shouted. "For God's sake, give me your hand!"

As she strained to reach her numb hands in the direction of his voice, she heard a faint musical sound. As first she thought it was a dream. Then it sounded louder. Over the howling of the storm, the Angelus rang out from the tower of St. Mary's Cathedral. Then the tolling stopped suddenly as if the bell's voice had been stilled by a brutal hand.

Six o'clock. The great two-ton bell at St. Mary's rang the Angelus every day at six o'clock. Yet already the sky was as black as night.

"Your hand," Michael shouted steadily. She groped blindly toward the sound. Suddenly his fingers touched hers, then closed around her wrist, jerking her arm painfully. "Swim," he ordered. "Swim."

A lazy sense of hopelessness slowed her movements. What was the use? Why should she fight what was coming anyway, no matter what she did?

The driving force of the water combined with Michael's frantic tugging to carry her onto the door beside him.

"Hang on," he shouted so fiercely that she stared at him. This was a stranger. His coat had been ripped away by the wind. A gaping tear in his shirt revealed a muscular arm, sliced by a wound which was darkened around the edges with slowly oozing blood. Who was this sodden man whose hair hung darkly in his face and whose voice was harsh and demanding in her ears over the screaming of the wind?

In her rational mind she knew he was still Michael. She knew the only reason she hadn't drowned long ago was his angry insistence that she live. But what was he fighting for? Didn't he know they were as good as dead? The night howled above them and the water that tugged at their makeshift raft was spinning them both toward certain doom.

The door struck the floating wall of a building like a battering ram, sending shock waves through Darcy's aching body. As it splintered and sped on in pieces, Michael caught her by the arm, dragging her with him. By gripping the window frames, Michael clung to the wall. His body covered hers like a coat, pressing her tightly against the wet, reeking wood. For the first time since she could remember, she was warm, shielded from the icy waves by the protection of his body.

The warmth dulled her senses so that she seemed

only half awake. There in that warm torpor, she rode the raft with him, beyond thought or feeling.

The last thing Darcy remembered was the roof of a house that plunged by them. A very little boy, probably no more than three years old, lay on the roof, his hand nailed to the shingle while the waves surged around him. He seemed to sleep.

Darcy dimly felt herself drift in and out of consciousness. Time had stopped or become meaningless. Like her mother before her and Hildy in her spotless kitchen, Darcy, dazed and only half conscious, made lists.

She had left too many things undone.

Why hadn't she let her father know how deeply she loved him?

Where was Rose?

And what to do about Michael, poor Michael, whose strength and determination were all that lay between them both and the certain death that was visible all about them in the flashes of lightning?

Some time during those troubled hours, the wall struck something solid and held. She dimly registered the shock of the impact and clung to Michael's warmth with a dull determination. When she roused herself enough to stare around her, she thought at first she was dreaming. She saw, in the intermittent light, that their wall raft had wedged itself into a giant pile of debris, wood, trees, houses and the contorted bodies of the dead.

Michael, his voice hoarse, brushed her matted hair from her face and whispered softly, "Thank God, thank God."

Even the rain seemed to be lessening. Instead of driving against them like bullets, it simply fell steadily, pouring from the cover of Michael's body to stream in rivulets around her own, chilling her so that she nestled even closer to Michael's warmth. His strength, which had sustained them all those hours, was finally spent. His head drooped onto her shoulder. His cheek, pressed against hers, was as hard and cold as the waters of the gulf.

Darcy knew that Michael had fallen asleep when his body softened against hers. With her arms locked around both him and the window frame, she felt sleep close in on her with an exhaustion as heavy as a stone.

Now and then the howling of the wind broke through into the muffled darkness of Darcy's dreams. Such tangled dreams they were. Once she heard singing, wavering voices raised in some quiet hymn of praise to God. She saw her mother, wearing a white dress and clinging to her ribboned hat with one hand as she ran with a kite. As Darcy stared, her mother looked at her and laughed merrily. A dog who sounded like Buffy barked and she tried to call to him. No sound came from her lips even though her throat ached from the effort of calling his name.

A light appeared. It bobbled along cheerily past

where Darcy clung with Michael. She stared at it, following it with her eyes as it moved unevenly in the darkness.

For a wild moment, her heart leaped in her chest. Help had come! They would be rescued, led to safety and light! Then the light bobbed and spun and moved on. Her eyes followed it with dull astonishment. Only when it had passed into darkness did she realize she had been watching a kerosene lamp still burning in a cottage being carried along on the surface of the flood.

In her dream she was rocking. After being so long at rest, the movement was welcome. The motion reminded her of being with her father out on the bay in a small rowboat. He smiled at her as he released one oar to draw her attention toward Pelican Island. She had laughed with delight as she watched a pod of dolphins leap into the air and dive to leap again.

The gentle motion became more urgent. It was not a rocking but a tugging. She wakened with a start. The raft shifted restlessly beneath them as if it were a trapped creature struggling to be free. As she tried to figure out what was happening, the black clouds parted, letting the moon's clear light through for a swift moment.

The water was receding. It was dropping swiftly, being sucked back toward the gulf with the same incredible force that had driven it ashore. The warmth was gone. She gasped, her mind instantly filled with horror stories of people and houses that had survived the flooding of the island only to be pulled back into the depths of the gulf and lost forever when the racing water returned to the sea.

"No," she cried, gripping Michael's arm to waken him. He groaned and pulled away from her so roughly that she had to take a fresh grip on his wet body. The flood was tugging at their wall, rocking it loose from its mooring. If they didn't escape it, they would surely be swept out to sea with it.

"Michael!" she screamed. "Michael!"

He opened his eyes to stare at her groggily. Then he glanced up to where the full moon rode in and out of the layers of dark cloud cover.

"The moon," he cried in a tone of delight. "The storm is over."

"It's *not* over," she cried desperately. "You've got to wake up. We have to get away."

"I don't understand," he murmured, shaking his head.

"The eye of the storm has passed," she told him frantically. "Now the gulf will take its water back the way it came, pulling us back with it." As she spoke, the shell of a cottage broke loose from the debris. Caught in the swift flood, it rode the dark torrent toward the gulf, spinning giddily as it raced along.

The moon was the only paleness in that dark world. All around them, the wall they clung to, the debris locked against it, even their own bodies were covered with a thick layer of mud. The retreating water was leaving a thick, oily deposit of a reeking, sticky slime in its wake.

The truth struck Michael with such sudden force that he gasped. He echoed Darcy's own anguished cry of "No," and braced himself against her. As he did, the wall, slick with mud, swung loose to slide on the sickening, receding water, gathering speed as it raced toward the gulf.

As the wall quickened in its progress, Michael caught Darcy around the waist. The darkness around them was only once in a while lit by the fugitive moon. When this happened, Darcy could identify many of the objects hurtling along on the face of the water, buggies, pieces of lumber, furniture, all the trappings of man along with the bodies of their owners. Michael's arm tightened around her as he stared with narrowed eyes into the blackness. His voice came low and persuasive. "Be ready, Darcy. Tense yourself and be ready. We'll only get one chance." He paused and caught a deep breath.

"Listen to me, Darcy. When I say jump, *jump*."

Tensed as she was from Michael's command, Darcy didn't notice at first that the wall they were traveling on had begun to tilt. Just the act of keeping her grip on the window frame took all her strength. This effort failed all at once, so suddenly that before she realized it, her own sodden weight had pulled her hands free and she was sliding. She tried to scream, to call to Michael, but there was no time. She slid deep into the icy water, kicking frantically at the debris beneath her. Her feet struck something solid and she flailed to the surface, gasping for air. Once there, she clutched wildly in the swirling water for anything solid to cling to.

At first it felt like a buggy whip, limber and frail and sleek with slime. Then the prickles of its damaged needles stung her hands. A salt cedar tree. She had caught the branch of a salt cedar tree, the only tree both hardy and flexible enough to take the punishment of salt spray and wind. She clung to it desperately, clawing along its branch until she reached the trunk. But where was Michael? When she called out to him, the wind whipped the words from her mouth, carrying them to sea.

If only the moon could break through so she could see. She strained to see anything of sense in the thundering darkness around her. But the moon was no help. It skulked like a fugitive, only now and then exposing its presence as a gleaming haze barely visible through the looming cloud cover.

Michael could not be lost, not after all he had done, all they had gone through together. She couldn't even bear the thought. The water kept receding, returning to the gulf at an almost unbelievable speed. She knew the moment the level of the water dropped beneath the limb where she clung. A sudden heaviness overwhelmed her. The very water that had threatened her life had also lightened the burden of her drenched clothing and her exhausted body. She fought tears from the fatal tiredness that clawed at her limbs.

"Michael," she called again without hope or conviction. But still she kept calling until her voice was only a painful rasp in her throat. Finally, completely despairing, she clung to the rough trunk of the swaying tree and wept.

Chapter Nine

Sunday, September 9, 1900, at dawn

THE light wakened Darcy, but only slowly. Her first consciousness was pain. Her entire body ached as if she had been ruthlessly beaten. The skin of both her face and arms was raw where it had come in contact with the rough surface of the tree trunk she was clinging to. Her head throbbed miserably and she had never been so thirsty in her life.

After the pain came a rush of horror. She was almost naked. The blouse of her dress had been wholly torn away, leaving her with only a cotton camisole with a ruffled front and her ragged knee-length pantalettes. Even these were streaked with filth and she had lost both shoes.

And she was alone.

The light was confusing. Far off in the west the moon still hung low in the sky, a full moon, its face faintly shadowed but its light brilliant on the restless waters of the gulf. In the east, bands of color wove through the pale clouds like ribbons. Their colors reminded Darcy of the delicate shades lining the conch shell that Angela had carried so carefully home from the beach only the day before.

The day before.

How could one single day — less than a day even — have held so much destruction and horror and death?

She thrust the thought of Angela away. She must not let herself think about anything but where she was and what she must do next. Most of all she must not let herself think of Michael, who had saved her life only to be swept to his own death.

She concentrated on the confusing sky. It grew lighter in the east by the moment. Dawn was coming. That was all. Dawn was coming and the retreating moon would soon be gone. And there was nothing but the black slime of desolation as far as she could see.

The salt cedar tree she clung to was one of several in a grove. A few yards away stood another grove partly hidden from her by a massive heap of debris. She had lodged near the top of the tree, several feet above the littered beach. The foliage was tattered and some of the lower branches had been torn away, but the limb where she clung was strong.

From this height, she could see relatively far. If it had not been for the giant piles of rubbish here and there along the beach, she thought she might be able to see forever. To the east the littered beach stretched open as far as she could see. Here and there a broken foundation jutted out of the mud but there were no houses at all, and no sign of human life. Twisting, she looked north to where the city should be. She searched for familiar landmarks, the steeples of churches, the tower of the city hall. If any of these still stood, they were hidden from her by the scattered walls of debris, shattered houses, lumber, and the twisted bodies of the dead. A fifty-foot-high wall of destruction loomed between her and what had been Galveston.

The silence of death hung in the air. Even the waves that nudged the mingled litter and corpses against the shore were quiet and the sky was empty of gulls.

She braced herself against the tree and buried her face in her hands. She couldn't look. It was hard enough to breathe the morning air heavy with the stench of the slime; she didn't have to look, too.

At first she thought the faint sound was the cry of a bird. When it came again, she recognized Michael's voice calling her name. For a moment, she was certain that she was dreaming. Hadn't her mind played tricks on her before? Hadn't she seen her dead mother alive and laughing during the fury of the storm?

When she heard the sound the third time, she gasped and cried out, looking around desperately. Michael couldn't have been saved. It was impossible. Yet even as the thought crossed her mind, she heard his voice again, nearer this time. Within moments he emerged from behind a pile of litter that partially obscured a nearby grove of salt cedar trees. She felt as if her heart would explode with relief as he slogged toward her through the mire.

She tried to climb down from her perch. The rough branches cut into her bare feet. Her pantalettes snagged and caught on the rough broken limbs. With trembling fingers she tried to undo them.

Once he saw her, Michael began to run toward her. By the time she worked the fabric free of the twigs, he was there at the base of the tree, holding his arms up to help her down. His clothing had fared little better than her own. His jacket and coat were all the way gone. His trousers hung in shreds about his knees. All he needed was a knife in his belt and a scarf around his head to look like one of Jean Lafitte's pirates, who had long ruled this very island.

But pirates didn't cry. Tears coursed down Michael's blackened face as he took her in his arms with a groan.

She didn't even try to understand the words he murmured against her throat as he clung to her. Her own relief exploded in her chest in a confused combination of joy and tears.

"I knew I had lost you," she cried. "I can't believe you are saved."

"It wasn't my doing," he said, still holding her. "As I slid from the wall, an old man grabbed my arm. He and another man pulled me into the branches of that strange little tree."

She glanced toward the grove and frowned. "Where are those men now?"

His tone was heavy. "Gone before I came to," he said. "I pray that they woke up and left safely. There were two of them, an old man and his son."

He looked at the massive bulwark of rubbish and then up and down the beach. "Do you know where we are?"

She shook her head. "Only in a general way. There are no landmarks left that I can see."

He took her hand. "It can't be as bad as it looks, Darcy. Come, I'll take you home."

Darcy forced herself not to think of the black mire she walked in. Her feet and ankles sunk into it. It was clammy and clung to her flesh like grease. Once she and Michael passed the largest mountain of reeking debris, Michael stared back at it a moment. "That monster probably saved a lot of lives besides ours. It served as a breakwater to shield some of the city. As for us, if we hadn't been lodged on it through the worst of the receding water, we wouldn't have made it."

Once they were on the other side of the barrier, she realized the truth of his words. On the north side of it, some houses still stood, their chimneys gone, porches blown away but the structures firm. They stood like stripped bathers in pools of water. Many other houses had been blown from their foundations to crush their neighbors' dwellings, but here and there walls still stood on their foundations with some promise of life.

Beyond them toward the high part of the city, the houses grew denser. But still she saw no landmarks to give her a clear sense of where they were. Michael and Darcy were not alone. Others besides themselves had left their shelters to stagger along the streets and peer at the faces of the dead, looking for their own.

Later Darcy realized that she could not have survived that morning's journey except for Michael's wisdom. Later she heard stories of people who had gone wholly mad that Sunday morning when they faced the enormity of the disaster or came upon the lifeless form of a mate or a child.

Michael kept her from that. When she stumbled and nearly fell at the sight of a dead child floating in a roadside ditch, he caught her almost roughly by the arms. "You must not look. You must not think. Save your strength for those you can help."

Although many of the homes they passed were terribly damaged, some still stood on their foundations. When Darcy saw the old Menard house up ahead, she quickened her steps.

"Michael," she cried. She seized his hand and pulled him along. "That's where the police chief, Ketchum, lives. Now I know where we are."

When she glanced toward the house as they passed, he spoke to her roughly. "Don't look, Darcy. Don't look."

He wasn't quick enough. She had glimpsed the sprawling corpses, at least eight or ten of them, tumbled like cordwood around the lawn beneath the giant live oak trees.

She swallowed hard, fought the hot tears behind her eyes and pulled at his hand. "Come this way, come quickly."

Three of the neighboring houses were wholly gone from their foundations. The carriage house from across the street had been lifted and hurled into her father's house. The roof and the whole attic and upstairs seemed to have been crushed by this blow before the carriage house had come to rest at a crazy angle toward the rear of the house. Tears rushed to Darcy's eyes as she ran toward the front porch, whose roof tilted onto the floor like a rakish hat.

Michael caught her hand and pulled her around to face him. "Expect the worst," he said. "Move carefully and expect the very worst."

A rush of sudden furious resentment rose in her chest. "Stop that!" she cried. "Don't try to tell me that Hildy is dead, that Rose isn't here. Isn't it enough that so much has been lost? Let me hope a little, if only for a minute."

His eyes were gentle on hers. "Make it easy on yourself. Just don't hope too much," he insisted.

Since the front door was crushed beneath the roof of the porch, Michael and Darcy crept gingerly along the porch, looking for some way to enter the house. The storm shutters had been torn from the parlor windows. Darcy and Michael climbed in carefully past the shards of broken glass. The house reeked of the same filth that coated the outside, making the floors as slippery as ice.

Michael caught Darcy's arm. "Watch!" he said. "There's a great gaping hole there in the floor."

Still holding her arm, he stared at the hole thoughtfully. "Darcy," he said, after a minute. "That hole wasn't made by the storm." He knelt beside it. "Look, it was hacked out by some tool, a hatchet I'd guess."

"But why would anybody do that?" she asked, then stopped. "Yes," she cried. "I'd forgotten. I've heard of people doing that before."

"Simple engineering," he said, rising. "Opening the windows and hacking holes in the floor for the water to run through a house might save it. The weight of the water filling the house could possibly make it too heavy for the wind to carry it away."

"But where is everybody? Then where could they go?" Darcy asked in anguish.

"Whoever did this understands storms," he assured her. "I'd say they knew where to take shelter."

Circling the hole, Darcy walked carefully through the parlor and into the foyer. The rugs were gone, the room bare of all but the most trivial pieces of furniture. A black line of slime marked where the water had climbed to the high ceilings and eaten away the ornamental molding that had been her mother's great pride.

"There's a hole in the foyer floor, too," Michael said with satisfaction.

Darcy stared at the ruined ceiling. If the water had entirely filled this room, Hildy must have sought refuge upstairs, possibly in the shallow high-pitched attic beneath the roof. The stairs were half shattered, with only the banister clinging to the inside wall. Darcy gripped the newel post and called into the darkness upstairs. "Hildy? Rose?"

Her voice echoed in the silence.

"They've gone somewhere," Michael assured her. "They've found shelter. They may be in one of those big houses we passed back there."

Darcy shook her head to caution him to silence. She circled the great gaping hole in the floor of the dining room and stared around the kitchen. "Hildy," she shouted with all her strength. "Rose!"

No human voice answered, but from somewhere in the darkness above them came a faint bark.

Darcy froze. "Buffy," she cried. "Buffy's up there somewhere." She started for the stairs but Michael caught her arm.

"You've got to be careful. Water leaves things balanced like a house of cards. A single wrong move and it can all fall down."

Then he looked at her, took her hand, and nodded. "All right. I know when I'm beaten. We'll go up together."

She wanted to race, to run up the stairs. If Buffy was there, Hildy could be, too. Even Rose might be there. At the top of the stairs she paused and called again. Strangely, the dog's bark seemed farther away and more muffled than before.

"It's not coming from inside this house," Michael decided aloud. "Let's go outside and try."

Darcy raged with impatience but knew better than to try to move hastily through the shattered rooms. Once outside again, they circled the building. Michael stared up at the neighbor's carriage house embedded at the back of the roof of the Dunlop house. The wooden storm shutters were tightly closed, showing no sign of life. There seemed no earthly way to get up there except by flying.

"You wait," he told Darcy. "Let me go see."

She ignored him. As soon as he crouched to creep under the angle of the broken wall where the carriage house had been driven by the wind, she bent almost double to follow him.

Once on the other side she shouted again, "Buffy!"

The animal's delirious bark was loud and very near but still above them. "Hildy," Darcy called, her voice almost drowned by tears.

A rattle sounded above them. The shutters on the back side of the carriage house swung open. Hildy appeared in the opening, her eyes wide and streaming tears.

"My baby," she cried. "My baby."

Buffy clawed at the ledge beside Hildy, wriggling

so madly that he almost pitched himself out of the window at Darcy.

"Is there a way up?" Michael called.

Hildy nodded and disappeared. When she returned, she began to feed a filthy, wet rope ladder out the window. When it had dropped to sway within a foot or so of the ground, Darcy seized it and began to climb.

Michael had more difficulty managing the rope ladder than Darcy did. Not only was he a lot heavier, but not everyone could be the child of a seafaring man.

While the air in the upper room of the carriage house smelled musty and damp, the main scent was a stable smell, the mingled odors of hay and horses and neat's-foot oil, a sweet relief from the outside air. Except for the one they had entered through, all the windows were closed and shuttered. The place was twilight dark. After the brilliant daylight outside, Darcy's eyes became accustomed only slowly to the dimness. The room was small, typical quarters for a bachelor groom or stable man. A low cot stood along one wall and most of the rest of the space was taken up by an unidentified mountain, carefully covered by a great sheet of tarp. Darcy recognized the tarp as one her father had brought home from the harbor to cover their own carriage house while the roof was being mended after a storm.

Darcy bit back her questions during Hildy's tearful greeting. She peered into the darkness of the carriage house for some sign of Rose or her father.

Before she could ask, Hildy rose and went into the dark corner. She lifted the edge of the tarp and fished around under it. "You have to be hungry and thirsty," she said, her voice muffled by her position. She returned, carrying two cans and a can opener.

Hildy peered curiously at the cans. "We worked on the floors before we started moving the supplies," she explained. "By that time a lot of these labels got thoroughly soaked." She smiled back at them. "It's catch as catch can, I'm afraid. Whatever you open, you eat. I *think* this is fruit. I tried to keep the same kinds of food together but it was a little hectic there at the end."

She chattered on as she opened the cans and handed them to Darcy and Michael. "Fruit's the best because it's got a lot of liquid. And the sugar peps you up."

Darcy's can held peaches. She swallowed the sweet, cool juice greedily. Only when it was gone did she eat the slick golden wedges of fruit. They tasted so good that tears of delight rose to her eyes.

"Not fruit, manna from heaven," Michael said. His can held pear halves, which were gone long before Darcy finished hers. Hildy offered to open him another can, but Michael shook his head. "Better to take it slowly," he said.

"When did you two last eat?" Hildy asked.

"Noon yesterday," Michael said, glancing around.

"Surely you didn't get all this up here by yourself."

Hildy looked startled. "Gracious, no. Peter and Miss Rose did the most of it."

Darcy leaped in. "Where are they now?"

"Looking for your father," Hildy said. "Peter went out early, just at dawn. He got a report that your father's ship had been blown from the harbor over onto Pelican Island. He and Rose went back to see what they could find out."

She turned to Michael. "How thoughtless we are. Here I go on and on about us. Tell me about the Mortons, Angela — "

Darcy shook her head. "We came straight here. Michael saved my life, Hildy, over and over again."

Hildy's eyes filled with instant tears and she groped for words. "Blessings, son, blessings forever. How can we thank you for keeping our girl safe and getting her back home?"

Michael grinned and winked at Darcy. "You told me to, Hildy, remember? I'm a man of my word."

He hesitated. "I do want to see about my family. You will be all right?" he asked Darcy.

"Oh yes, thank you, yes." She paused. "Oh, Michael, what can I do?"

"Stay here and be safe. I'll get back to you. I'll let you know how things are. Don't worry about anything else. Just wait for Peter to bring word of your father."

"But I feel I should go with you," she protested, her mind suddenly full of Angela's terror. She knew better, but a superstitious shiver went up her spine as she thought of Mrs. Morton's awful fear of storms.

"Go with him?" Hildy asked, her voice rising almost to a shriek. It was as if she really *saw* Darcy for the first time. She ran to the cot, pulled off the rumpled sheet that covered it, and threw it around Darcy. "Tramping all over this island in your underwear? Not on your life, you don't."

Darcy fought the sheet awkwardly as she braced the ladder for Michael to climb down. At the bottom, he held the ropes in both hands and tugged, looking up at her. His whisper was carefully modulated to keep Hildy from hearing.

"Now you *have* to be engaged to me. Isn't that the rule since we've spent the night together?"

She stared at him open-mouthed, then felt the scarlet blush travel up her face. She almost called him down but didn't want to explain her words to Hildy.

Anyway, he wasn't a bad man, as she would have told him. He was good and brave and wonderful.

And she loved him.

Chapter Ten

Sunday, September 9, 1900

HILDY wouldn't let Darcy go back into the house alone to get her clothes. As they left, Buffy barked frantically from the window of the carriage house, begging to go along. "You stay here and guard," Hildy called to him.

When Darcy chuckled, Hildy grinned at her. "The truth is that it's hard enough to get my own body up and down that waggling rope ladder without hauling that squirming fellow along. And *this* makes me feel like a burglar," she added, as they climbed into the parlor through the broken window.

"I can't believe all this work you did," Darcy said as they entered the library.

"It's not a patch to the work we have to do now," Hildy grumbled.

"But how did you get it all done?" Darcy asked.

"Moving the furniture, taking up rugs." She nodded toward the hole in the middle of the room. "Cutting those holes."

"I wasn't working alone," she reminded Darcy. "Rose came back about a half hour after you and Michael left. And Peter did the man's share, as he always does. It broke my heart seeing him hack holes in that beautiful parquet floor, but he knew what he was doing." Then she started up the stairs, not meeting Darcy's eyes. "It was good we had *something* to keep us busy. We sure were not going to leave without you and the captain."

"Oh, Hildy," Darcy said, suddenly overwhelmed with how it must have been to wait, not knowing, all that day and night through the howling wind and pounding water.

"I'd guess you and your friend didn't have any picnic, either," Hildy told her. Her eyes questioned Darcy as she spoke.

Picnic, Darcy's mind echoed. What could she say? It was over. Wasn't that really enough?

"We got through it," she said, touching Hildy's arm as she spoke.

Although the floodwater had risen only halfway up the second floor, the driving rain had battered the upper floors, too, making its way inside at every opportunity. A paste of black soot fanned down from the mouth of the fireplace in Darcy's bedroom. Chunks of fallen plaster littered the floor where the roof had leaked, letting the water flow through.

"This place is a sight," Hildy said with disgust in

her voice. "Some of the roof slates must have blown off." She tugged the closet door open and began flipping through the rack looking for dry garments.

Slates.

Darcy stood very still, shivering at the sound of the word. Hildy must have sensed her distress because she turned to stare at her. The older woman crossed the room in swift steps and put her arms around Darcy. "What's wrong, love? What happened?"

Would it make her own gruesome memories any easier to bear if she shared them with Hildy? She clung to the older woman, warmed by the tangible love in Hildy's grip.

Was she ever going to be able to think straight again? Instead of being there with Hildy in that mutilated room, Darcy's mind slid back to a distant time. She had been a very little girl, maybe four or five, playing with jacks and a ball on the porch. A seagull swayed in from the beach and flew directly toward the house. She remembered looking up to watch it in total fascination. It was small with body feathers as white as a freshly starched pinafore and long, gracefully bent wings. Its delicate, neat head was hooded with black, a shining darkness in complete contrast to the color of its other feathers.

Before she had been able to catch her breath, the gull, apparently confused by its reflection in the plate glass of the parlor window, had flown straight into the glass. It fell with a sickening thud on the porch floor beside Darcy.

Darcy had leaped up, screaming for her mother. She cried helplessly as her mother picked up the bird and cradled it in her hands. "I'll take it out to the stable," her mother told her. "Maybe it's only stunned and will fly again."

Darcy didn't see the gull again. When she asked her mother about it, her mother almost repeated the same words. "A lot of times they are only stunned and can fly again."

In her heart Darcy had known the gull had not flown. Somehow, not having its death put into words made it easier for her to bear.

Darcy shut her eyes against her memory of the slate slicing the man's neck like Hildy's cleaver. She chose her words carefully as she answered.

"A lot of slates blew loose and were flying around during the worst of the storm," she told Hildy quietly.

Outside, the tenor of Buffy's barking had changed. It had become louder and more urgent and once in a while he whimpered. Hildy moved swiftly. "That'll be our people," she said, thrusting a white shirt and a damp black skirt at Darcy. "These will have to do for now. Let's go see what they've learned."

Peter and Rose were coming around the end of the house as Hildy and Darcy climbed out the parlor window onto the porch. Rose was carrying a bundle with both hands. At the sight of Darcy, she cried out, thrust the bundle at Peter, and ran awkwardly through the slime to her cousin.

As Darcy caught her in her arms, the bundle moved in Peter's grip and began to wail in the high, choking tones of a very young infant.

"What in the world?" Hildy cried, bracing herself against the porch balcony.

"I tried to tell her a hundred times," Peter protested, struggling awkwardly with a squirming child.

Hildy moved swiftly down the steps and across the yard to take the bundle from Peter. Once its face was uncovered the child quit protesting and lay quietly along Hildy's arm, staring up at her with wide, blue eyes. It was a round-faced, chubby infant, with a fine cap of twisted reddish curls. Wearing only the ragged remnants of a nightshirt, the baby's legs were free to pummel Hildy's chest as it stared back at her. "But," Hildy stammered, "whose child is this?"

Rose had left Darcy's embrace to run to Hildy's side. "I heard him crying," she said. "We were on our way back from town and I heard crying from under a fallen house."

"She dug him out from under a pile of broken boards and muck, she did. Look at her!" Indeed, Rose's dress was black with slime and only at that moment did Darcy realize that the child was wrapped in her cousin's fine lawn petticoat.

"And its mother?" Hildy asked, her tone hesitant.

Peter shook his head with his lips held grimly together.

Rose lifted the child from Hildy's arms and braced him against her shoulder. Her words came swiftly like those of a child trying to talk a parent into something that she's sure she's not going to be allowed to do. "There's all that food of yours, Hildy, and you know he's hungry." She lifted the child back from her shoulder. "Look how he chews on his fist. He's starving!"

"But his family — " Hildy began.

"Them that was there was past saving," Peter said quietly. "There's scenes out there that scald a man's soul. But Rose is right about one thing. That little fellow is like to eat himself up if he's not fed soon."

Hildy rocked back a little on her heels and stared off across the street to where the once-proud house of their neighbors was now a pile of broken wood and shattered plaster covered by mud. Darcy looked at Peter and he shrugged. They both knew that Hildy made a decision swiftly, silently, and all by herself.

Hildy turned back to them briskly. "You go first, Darcy, and Rose will hand up the child. We need to get some nourishment into him first thing. While we're at it, Peter, I want you to go back into that kitchen. Mind you be careful where you step. There's a full pantry shelf of clean dishcloths. We best start getting them out to dry now. If you'll just hang them on the wash line — " She stopped, shook her head and started again. "Where's my head? There's no wash line left. Just find clean places the sun can get to them."

With the infant hungrily gulping canned milk from a teaspoon in Rose's arms, Hildy started back down the ladder.

"I can go help Peter," Darcy told her.

Hildy shook her head. "Best you wait up there with Rose," Hildy told her. "I want to have a word with Peter."

Darcy waited until Hildy reached the bottom, then started down after her. "I want to know about Papa, too," she said.

Hildy glared at her but didn't insist.

"It's no pretty story," Peter told Darcy with warning in his tone, and a look of disapproval because she insisted on staying while he reported to Hildy.

"I spent no *pretty* night on this island," Darcy said, deliberately staring him down. "Now tell us, Peter, what did you learn?"

"Things didn't go well at the wharf," he began. He cleared his throat and scrubbed at the mire at his feet with a boot. "No one can tell me just when the *Sojourner* broke loose, but she was gone by the time the storm wave struck a little after six."

"She was still there a little after noon," Darcy told him. "She was shut up tight and braced with all kinds of lines. Michael and I waited a while, hoping to see Papa. I decided he was riding the storm out down in the cabin. What was this about the *Sojourner* being sighted on Pelican Island?"

"That was the first word. Now nobody is sure. Some say that could have been Simpson's *Hard Times* that cast off from Pier 19 about two-thirty. The boats look alike, both being two-masted and about the same length."

"We need to get a boat," Darcy said. "We'll go to Pelican Island and find out for sure."

Peter shook his head. "That's easier spoke than managed. There's no craft to speak of surviving. Mayor Jones met this morning at the Tremont Hotel with a bunch of the main men in town. With all this death and destruction, the city is going to need help from the mainland. The mayor sent over a committee of men in Moody's steam launch, the *Pherabe*, to get the word out about what's happened here. That launch was one of the few crafts that survived, and it's gone now."

Hildy studied him, then stepped back to lean against the side of the house. "How bad is it, Peter? How bad is it really?"

Peter shook his head. "Nobody knows for sure. We're cut off from everything. The bridge is gone. The railway's under water. No telephones, no telegraph, no water or electricity. Some say five hundred people died, others put it closer to a thousand. There's not a church left undamaged. St. Mary's Orphanage is only a few scattered bricks, and some guess that more than three thousand homes were blown away."

He sighed. "Right now I need to eat a bite and

go back downtown. They've asked every able-bodied man to help dig out the trapped and bury the dead."

"But what about Papa?" Darcy wailed.

Hildy laid a hand on her arm. "We'll find him, Darcy. Just have faith."

"Peter," Darcy said after a moment, "you didn't see Mr. Morton or Angela, did you?"

His face twisted in sudden pain. "Matter of fact, I did talk with Mr. Morton, down by the Strand. Seems his missus was caught out in it and never came home. He was still looking for some word of her."

Darcy stared at him a moment, then straightened her back.

How foolish she had been to think that when the storm was over that would be the end of it. It was all just beginning. It was a nightmare that had survived the night and might never go away.

Michael's voice echoed in her mind, his tone rough and demanding; Michael ordering her to save her strength for the living, the people she could help.

"Peter," she pleaded. "Where can I go to look for Papa?"

Hildy stared at her, aghast, but Peter shook his head. "Wherever your papa is," he said, "the *Sojourner* is with him."

She studied his face, so visibly aged in the last day. He was right, of course. Her father would have stayed with the ship if there was a single other man on it beside himself. The black memory of the corpses spinning past her into the darkness of the gulf flooded her mind. If he had taken the schooner from the port he might never be found. From the lines in Peter's face, she guessed he had faced the same terrible possibility. Yet he meant to respond to the mayor's call for able-bodied men. Peter, able-bodied? With his damaged leg and uneven walk?

Back upstairs, Rose had laid the sleeping child on the cot and sat silently watching him. Eating had brought a flush to his cheeks. His mouth twitched in a vagrant smile as Darcy came in and looked at him. "What did you think you would do with him?" Darcy asked in a careful whisper.

Rose looked up, her eyes suddenly brimming with tears. "I guess I didn't think very far ahead," she said, her tone tearfully apologetic. "I only thought about getting him out of there, of saving his life." She caught a deep breath and looked down at him. "We were too late for so many others, including his mother."

As Peter finished his cold meal of corned beef hash, apple sauce and whole hominy, Darcy sat down with Hildy. "I need to leave when Peter does," she said quietly.

Hildy's back stiffened and she started to protest. Darcy shook her head. "Listen to me," she insisted, hearing Michael's firm orders behind her own voice. "Surely soon the people on the mainland will know what has happened here and they'll come over. Until there are boats, we can't search for Papa. I need to go where I *know* I can help. I'll take some cans of food along in case the Dunlops didn't have your foresight about laying in supplies. If Angela's mother has been found, I'll celebrate that with her. If she hasn't, she'll need greater comfort than I can bring. But I can at least try."

Hildy stared at her dully. Silent tears formed in the older woman's eyes and flowed unheeded down the ridges of her cheeks. She didn't even raise a hand to wipe them away.

"Hildy," Darcy begged, "please don't cry. Believe me, I'm not doing this to worry you, or make you unhappy."

"I know that," Hildy said, turning away. She sniffed and smudged at her tears with the back of her hand. "I just wanted you to be young and happy and carefree for a little bit longer. Of course we'll send food. Would you like Rose to go along with you?"

Darcy shook her head and smiled. "She's better off where she is."

Darcy had walked those few blocks to Angela's house since she was a child, first with her mother, later with Hildy, and for the last few years alone at appropriate hours. She would have said she could walk those blocks in her sleep. She had never expected to walk them in a nightmare.

The howling of the wind the day before had been replaced by a sadder sound. The city was alive with people searching for their dead. From all directions she heard the scrape of shovels and the voices of men lifting the shattered houses from the injured who were trapped below. Among the low, human sounds of cries for help and wails of grief came the sudden explosive sound of gunfire, not once but over and over, and then silence.

Darcy stood rooted to the street in astonishment. A man shoveling at the litter of a house stood up and looked at her. He made a face and, pressing the palm of his hand against his back, he straightened. His face was twisted with hate. "Buzzards," he said fiercely. "There're always buzzards."

She gasped and looked up at the sky. "You are a young one, aren't you?" he asked bitterly. "I mean human buzzards. By now they'll be looting this town like it was an open bank. There's no cure for a looting human buzzard but gunshot."

She stared at him, tightened her hand on the bag of canned goods and almost ran the rest of the way to the Morton house.

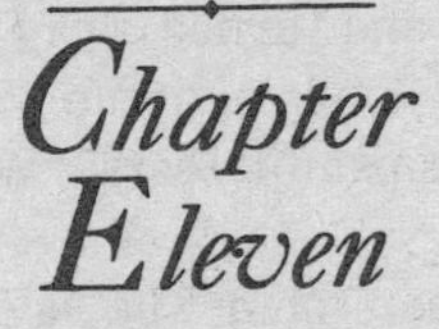

Chapter Eleven

Sunday, September 9, 1900

THE Morton house had fared better than their own. Though the black line of mud had left a line on the second-story paint, the porch had stood firm. The shutters had been torn away and the windows stared black and eyeless, emptied of glass. Only the chimney and a little of the roof had blown away.

When the bell didn't sound, Darcy rapped sharply on the door with her knuckles. She heard hollow footsteps on the exposed wooden floor. The door swung open and Mr. Morton, his face dark with pain, looked down at her. To her astonishment, she heard, back in the house, the murmur of women's voices and a baby crying.

"Oh, my dear," he said fervently. He took Darcy's hand and started to pull her inside. Then, as if remembering, he released her hand, stepped out on the porch beside her and closed the door behind himself. "Some of our neighbors sought shelter here during the storm," he explained. "You can't know how relieved I was when Michael told me he had delivered you safe at home. And how much it means just to see you. I should have known that you would come when my Angela needed you the most." He burst into tears and turned away.

That at least explained the voices Darcy had heard but not his painful tears. "Where is Angela?" she asked.

"She's up in her room," he said. "Come. May I take your things?"

Numbly Darcy handed him the canvas bag. Its weight obviously startled him. "My dear, what are you carrying?"

Suddenly she was embarrassed. Here she was, bringing food to the door of one of Galveston's most prosperous builders. "Food," she stammered. "Hildy always stocks a lot of canned goods and we weren't sure you'd have anything here to eat."

"Bless you," he said, opening the bag and peering in. "After feeding our guests the pantry here is bare."

He stopped and looked toward the kitchen. "If you don't mind, I'll take this into the women and come back. I'd like a moment with you alone."

She heard delighted cries from behind the closed door and then he returned. She wanted to ask about Michael but held the words back from shyness. Mr. Morton returned and gestured for Darcy to follow him into the deserted parlor. For a long moment he only stood where Angela's piano had been, his eyes closed. Then he spoke.

"You don't know, do you, my dear?"

Darcy shook her head slowly. He must not say what she was dreading to hear. He must not.

Mr. Morton's words came out very sluggishly, with infinite care. "We found Angela's mother. She had taken refuge with the friend she went shopping with. The roof collapsed and every soul in the house was killed instantly. I can only give thanks for that, that she didn't know, she didn't suffer."

As Darcy struggled for words, he took both her hands, ignoring his own streaming eyes. "Don't try to say anything. I know you understand. Maybe only you, of all people, can speak to Angela. I can't reach her. Michael can't reach her. She's like a crazed creature."

Darcy nodded and turned to start upstairs to Angela's room. She was in the hall when he thought to follow her. "Darcy, my dear," he said, his tone remorseful. "In my own grief I have forgotten about others. How is your own family? All well?"

Maybe she was more like Hildy than she had realized. She had made one important decision when Hildy had mentioned the roof slate. Passing along her fear about her father wasn't going to lighten her own burden. Why should she add to anyone else's grief by talking about it?

She didn't look at Angela's father as she replied, fearing he might read the fuller truth written in her face. "All fine," she said, keeping her voice level. "We haven't seen Papa yet but we're sure he's somewhere on the *Sojourner* with his crew."

She felt his eyes on her back as she went on upstairs. Her feet felt as fragile as glass on the slippery bare wood.

Angela lay in darkness with the heavy drapes pulled shut. For a moment Darcy thought she might be sleeping, but as she paused in the doorway, Angela spoke.

"Go away."

When Darcy hesitated, she spoke again, this time with anger. "Go away. I don't want anything. I just want to be left alone."

As Darcy's eyes grew accustomed to the darkness, she realized that Angela, who lay curled tightly with her back to the door, couldn't possibly even know who was there. Darcy's impulse was to go to the windows and let the sunshine stream in. Instead she waited a moment and then identified herself. "It's me, Angela. It's Darcy."

Darcy didn't know what she expected but it wasn't a sudden storm of tears. When Darcy went to the bed and laid her hand on her friend's shoulder, Angela cried even harder and pulled herself roughly away.

"It's our fault, yours and mine," she sobbed. "We could just as easily have done those errands for her Friday. Those dance programs weren't *that* important. If we had, she'd be here right now. And forever." At that she burst into a fresh flood of tears.

Darcy looked at her in horror. Such a thought hadn't even crossed her mind. And it didn't make any sense at all. Why had Angela twisted the facts around to create this monstrous guilt?

When she stayed silent, Angela flipped over to face her. "We did it, the two of us. You know it as well as I, we the same as killed her."

Darcy crossed the room swiftly and pulled the drapes open, flooding the room with light. "That's ridiculous and you know it," she said, conscious that her voice was trembling dangerously.

Angela covered her eyes with her hands and wailed. "Get rid of that light," she shrieked. "Get out of here and leave me alone!"

"Go on, bring everyone in this house up here," Darcy told her. "Is that what you want? How dare you make a scene and wallow in your made-up guilt while your father swallows his grief to serve his neighbors, and this city is an open grave?"

Angela let her hands drop to stare at Darcy.

"It was you. You and your silly party, and having a big fit because of the change. I hope you're happy now. You the same as killed my mother."

Darcy stared at her friend in disbelief. Angela was obviously hysterical. Had she even been outside of this sturdy house since Darcy and Michael had dropped her here the day before? Had she seen the thousands of homes swept away by water and wind, the corpses floating in the street and heard the wails of trapped people crying for release? How *could* she know that no one was at fault, that her tragedy and those of all the others were an act of nature beyond anyone's control?

"Listen to me, Angela," Darcy commanded. "There *is* no guilt, not yours, not mine, not anyone's. Your mother was only one among thousands who perished in this storm. And your father told me what happened. It was quick and must have been painless. Believe me, Angela, few of your mother's dead friends had so easy a passing."

"What a liar you are! I can't believe you are even exaggerating *this*. It's a sin, and you're a selfish, heartless beast," Angela shouted at her. "Get out of my sight. I never want to see you again in my life — not ever. I wish I were dead myself."

She began to sob wildly. Darcy stared at her, feeling suddenly emptied and bleak. Was she being mean and heartless? Did she really believe the words she had spoken? Had her words only come from her own slowly spiraling terror over her father's fate?

A faint tapping at the door startled her.

"Go away," Angela called furiously. "I don't want to see anyone."

Darcy, her legs unsteady beneath her, went to the door and opened it. Seeing Michael looming above her in the dim hall unnerved her. He was no longer the pirate who had left her at the carriage house. He was wearing a laborer's clothing, rough trousers and an open-necked cotton shirt. This clothing was heavily soiled and his face was tight with the ravages of the past hours. More than anything she wanted to fly into his arms for comfort.

Instead, unable to deal with Angela wailing behind her, she pushed past Michael and ran down the stairs with a thundering heart. All she could think of was escape. She couldn't bear the sound of Angela's hysterical accusations or the confusion in Michael's face.

She flew through the foyer. The voices of the women in the kitchen almost drowned out the sound of Michael's voice calling her name. She ran heedlessly down the street, not caring that she splashed through standing puddles of the thick, greasy mud. She was crying in spite of herself, her tears spinning back to dampen the hair along her cheeks.

She only stopped running when a stitch in her chest bent her double with pain. She straightened and walked on carefully, concentrating on putting one foot carefully in front of the other to ease the pain underneath her heart.

The noise around her should have been sufficient to blot Angela's accusations out of her mind. The survivors still labored at their search for the dead. Men's voices echoed through the ruins as they shouted directions at each other. Lumber and metal being torn loose shrieked from the pressure of levers and axes. The air smelled of death and Angela's words battered Darcy's brain. "You the same as killed my mother. You the same as killed my mother."

She forced herself to concentrate on the few

things left around her that were familiar and comfortable enough to remind her that this was her beloved Galveston. She startled a sandpiper stalking along the street, hunting in puddles. Overhead the gulls swayed and screeched their inevitable complaints. She was almost home before her heart began to beat even halfway normally again.

She heard the sound of hammering as she circled the house. Buffy yapped happily at her from the carriage house window and she stopped in amazement. Hildy appeared from behind the ruins of the house next door, dragging a long wooden plank through the mire behind her.

"Come give us a hand," Hildy called. "This thing weighs a ton." It also smelled terrible and was nasty to touch, covered with thick, dark mud. Darcy forced herself to lift one end of the wood and drag it along behind Hildy. At Hildy's signal, she dropped it a couple of feet from another piece of wood about the same size.

"What are you doing with these?" Darcy asked, looking around fruitlessly for something to wipe her hands on.

"Building a ladder," Hildy said, panting a little. Then she smiled a little, as if amused at herself. "I collected some short pieces of wood to use for stairs first. Mostly because they were easier to handle. Peter had a hammer and some nails in the tool box he left in the kitchen." She paused. "How are things at the Morton's?"

Darcy stared at her for a moment. Was she going to fight being tongue-tied the rest of her life?

"The house was full of the homeless," she said, "so the food was greatly needed."

Hildy stood very still, her eyes apprehensive on Darcy's face. "And Mrs. Morton?" she asked. "Did they locate her?"

Darcy couldn't speak. When she only shook her head, Hildy studied her face for a long moment. Then she reached for Darcy and held her close a long time, murmuring something tearful that Darcy couldn't understand. Hildy's warmth was healing. When she released Darcy, the words came, though with difficulty.

"She died when the home of her friend collapsed. It was very quick. Mr. Morton is comforted that she didn't suffer."

"The dead are released," Hildy said, wiping angrily at her eyes. "The living do the suffering." She bent and picked up the hammer. "And Angela?" Hildy asked, handing Darcy a handful of nails.

"She isn't making any sense," Darcy said.

Hildy's glance was keen. "That's probably shock. Poor child, she has lived in such fear of this. Now, if you'll hand me those nails one at a time, I'll start hammering. I don't want anyone arguing with us about staying here as long as we want to."

"Whose business is it but our own?" Darcy asked.

"Nobody's," Hildy said shortly. "But some folks have already taken it into their heads that we should leave."

"That's ridiculous," Darcy said. "How would Papa know where to find us if we left?"

By twilight the ladder was finished, ready to lift into place. The sunset colors had faded completely from the sky when Peter returned, gray with fatigue. Hildy's search of the kitchen had yielded a spirit stove and some dry matches in a can.

"You'll need double sugar in that coffee," she told Peter. "The water tastes as bad as it smells."

He accepted the cup and drank deeply, holding it with both hands. In spite of the extra sweetening, he made a face at the brackish taste of the brew. "We won't be putting up with this foul water much longer," he said. "There's a great gang of men, maybe a hundred, repairing the waterworks to get it flowing again."

While Rose played happily with the baby on her lap, Hildy and Darcy made plans. The next morning they would clean the lower rooms, mend the floors and move some furniture back down from the upstairs. Once settled back into the house, Hildy assured her, things would swiftly get back to normal.

"You ladies give me a lot of confidence," Peter said from his corner. His words startled Darcy. Indeed, Hildy was no longer treating Darcy as a feckless child, but rather as an equal. This made her feel good and somehow important, but lonelier than ever.

Hildy's new confidence in her didn't extend to letting Darcy sleep alone in the damaged house.

Together with Peter, they hauled a mattress up the ladder into the carriage house. "Peter will take the cot," Hildy decreed, "and we'll share the other."

Rose's baby was genial. He seemed content to eat and sleep and coo softly at his fingers in the light of the kerosene lamp. Rose fell asleep first and then Hildy, with Peter dead to the world from exhaustion on the cot.

Darcy, who had never shared a room with anyone except when she was sick as a child, stirred restlessly a long time before finally getting up and making her way down the ladder. She sat on the bottom rung, staring into the stinking darkness. So many houses had been stripped away that she could clearly see the gulf gleaming silver under the nearly full moon. Here and there in the dark desolation that had been a city of almost forty thousand people, a lantern winked briefly and disappeared.

She had never really understood loneliness before. It was not so much a pain as an emptiness. Michael had sustained her through the agony of the storm and she would be grateful to him for this forever. But Hildy was right. The suffering was left to the living. And the absence of her father was an open wound. Where was the *Sojourner* and her father? Had they been driven inland by the force of the gulf or sucked out to sea in the retreat of the storm? Surely by the next day some boats from the mainland would make it to the island. Surely they would bring word of the ships that had been torn from the wharf.

The question came unbidden to her mind. Would it comfort her to learn that her father had perished quickly and without pain? Knowing the answer, she put her head on her lap and cried for both Angela and herself.

Chapter Twelve

Monday, September 10, 1900

PETER made quick work of mending the drain holes he had hacked in the floors of the downstairs rooms. "I'll try to do something about that staircase come morning," he said. "We've got to get those downtown streets cleared so that wagons can come with supplies."

When he had limped off toward town to put in his daily stint, Hildy whipped the spirit lamp down the ladder, set it on the kitchen counter and put a pan of cistern water on it to boil.

"What's that for?" Darcy asked. The little lamp couldn't possibly produce enough hot water for them to clean the filthy kitchen.

"To make this day bearable," Hildy told her. She rummaged in the cupboard and returned with a handful of spices, dark sticks of cinnamon, a handful of cloves and a great dry bay leaf, which she crumpled into tiny pieces and dropped into the water. Within minutes the air, which had been so foul that Darcy had wakened gagging, was filled with a spicy perfume.

"I don't think I ever appreciated you," Darcy told Hildy.

"That probably goes both ways," Hildy said as Darcy pushed the wire brush back and forth along the kitchen counter.

Within an hour Darcy's arms ached from the mopping and scrubbing, but her spirits were strangely lightened. How proud her father would be of them. She pushed away the dark thought that he might not swing through that door and see his house being put back in order.

Darcy was on her knees with the scrub brush when she heard Buffy's sharp bark of welcome outside. Her heart leaped with unreasonable joy, with the wild hope that her father had returned. Instead, she heard Mrs. Turner's question to Rose.

"For heaven's sake, Rose. Whose child is that?"

At Rose's lilting response, Darcy got up and looked her appeal to Hildy.

"She was here yesterday," Hildy whispered. "I had a feeling she'd be back. She wants us to move over and stay with her and Alex at her place until this house is repaired. The way she put it was more an order than an invitation. I got nowhere with her."

"Maybe I'll have better luck," Darcy said, hastily

brushing her hair out of her eyes and wiping her hands.

Mrs. Turner appeared in the doorway, her eyes widening with shock. "For heaven's sakes, Darcy," she cried. "You can't be scrubbing. That will ruin your skin!"

Her words might have been easier for Darcy to take if Mrs. Turner hadn't been perfectly turned out in her usual funereal black. Every hair was in place under a pert hat trimmed with a pale yellow silk rose. She was even wearing sleek leather gloves.

Darcy fought an impulse to hide her reddened hands behind her back as she forced a smile. "Good morning," she said brightly. "Don't worry. Skin will mend. Hildy and I are getting the house cleaned up for Papa."

Mrs. Turner's look of confusion was replaced by one of amazement. "How wonderful! I hadn't heard. Was the captain on his ship all that time?"

Darcy was trapped. When she looked at Hildy for help, Mrs. Turner caught the significance of the glance. She crossed the room swiftly and put her gloved hand on Darcy's arm. "I see, my dear," she said smoothly. Then, after the tiniest pause, she asked, "Would you do me the great favor of letting me speak with Hildy alone?"

"Please, Mrs. Turner. If your conversation has anything to do with me or my father, I'd rather stay."

The woman looked at her with disbelief, then

shrugged. "Very well, but you know as well as I do that your father would heartily disapprove of this aggressive attitude of yours."

Darcy felt a sudden surge of anger. There that woman went again! It wasn't bad enough that she acted as if she and Darcy's mother had been intimate friends; now she was acting as if she knew more about Darcy's own father than Darcy did.

Mrs. Turner turned away and spoke to Hildy regally as if Darcy were not even in the room. "I'm sure you don't realize how dire the circumstances are, Hildy. A large number of undesirable people have managed to get onto our island. Several looters have already been shot, houses have been broken into and stores robbed. The mayor has brought in the battery guard to protect the business district. He has asked that the city be put under martial law. He's already closed the saloons and gambling houses and sworn in temporary officers, but that doesn't make the city safe for women with small children here alone."

"We're not alone," Darcy broke in. "Peter is here with us every minute that he's not doing volunteer work cleaning streets downtown."

Mrs. Turner looked at her coldly. "Darcy, because of my affection for your late mother and my respect for your father, I will graciously ignore your rudeness to me. But I urge you to consider my offer seriously, now and later. You are welcome at my house, and will continue to be."

Darcy couldn't pretend a warmth she didn't feel,

but neither could she fail to say *something* when the woman continued to stare at her with an expression of angry disgust.

"Thank you very much, Mrs. Turner," she said. Only when the words were out did she realize how formal and final and almost snippish they sounded.

Mrs. Turner's reaction was not immediate. She stared at Darcy for a long, angry minute before she began to speak. When she did, her voice was lower and trembling with fury. "I shudder to think how your mother would feel about the way you are turning out, Darcy Dunlop. Oh, I don't blame the captain and Hildy here for indulging you the way they have. It's natural to pity a motherless little girl. But you have taken brazen advantage of them. It was bad enough when you were only spoiled and willful and selfish, with your constant parties and your distraction with fancy clothes and pleasure-seeking. But this coldness of yours is appalling. Have you once thought of poor Rose's family off there in Houston, not knowing if their precious child has lived or died? Have you thought of the heartbreak your carelessness about convention has brought Hildy here? The streak of meanness you have revealed is simply shocking."

At Hildy's strangled protest, the woman went on. "I know you don't like to hear the truth any more than this young lady does, Hildy, but *somebody* has to set her straight. Running around with her figure displayed for all to see like a loose street woman, fawning over that Yankee nephew of the Morton's and disappearing with him to be gone for hours without a chaperone." She paused. "Oh, don't think I didn't know that you were gone all day and all night, young lady. Alex and I only chanced to learn about *that* escapade when we made an arduous visit over here to offer our help. Do you have any idea of Hildy's agony as those hours continued to pass? Or do you care?"

"Escapade!" Darcy breathed in disbelief.

Mrs. Turner gripped her little black purse tighter, her dark eyes blazing. "Your hours are numbered, Darcy Dunlop. You have no assurance that your father survived this catastrophe. This very day the firemen are loading hundreds, maybe a thousand, souls on a barge to be towed out into the gulf for burial at sea—nameless, unidentified bodies. If your father does not return, and I pray fervently that he does, you will, as a minor, be the responsibility of this city. Then you, as well as that pitiful orphan your cousin is entertaining herself with, will be forced to conform to the rules of society." She shrugged. "There'll be no more camping out in a dangerous ruined house or making impudent remarks to your elders and betters."

When she turned and swept out, Darcy gripped her hands before her chest with a moan. She felt physically battered by the dreadful things the woman had said, the hatred in her voice.

Hildy let her breath out in a slow stream, almost like a whistle. Darcy, knowing that Hildy would try to comfort her, turned and started out of the kitchen. No amount of gentle coddling could heal the pain of Mrs. Turner's searing words.

"Darcy," Hildy called after her. "Darcy, love."

"I'll be right back," Darcy told her. "I just need a little time alone, Hildy. I'll be back."

Without a second thought, she passed through the hall and started upstairs for her own room. It had been her refuge for as long as she could remember. Never mind the great gaping hole in the wall and the water spots staining her beautiful rug and furnishings. There she could be herself — not that dreadful person Mrs. Turner had described in her scalding words. And from there she could see the face of the gulf, smooth and serene and beautiful.

But if Hildy knew where she was going, she'd have an argument. She couldn't deal with that.

Remembering Michael's warning, she went up carefully, clinging to the banister side of the stairs. The thought of Michael brought a fresh rush of pain. Michael. How did Michael see her? Was Alex's mother's view only a distorted mirror or did she appear to be all those ugly things to other people, too? Angela's bitter words still rang in her mind. Even if she took away the hysterical business about her guilt, Angela's other accusations were left — mean, selfish. Only a day before she had been so close to Michael. Now, after seeing herself through Mrs. Turner's eyes, she wasn't sure she would ever be able to face him again.

She crept very quietly, painfully conscious of Hildy down there waiting to comfort her. Comfort or spoil, what *was* it really?

By the time she reached the upstairs hall, she was fighting tears. All she wanted in the world was to throw herself across her own bed and cry as she had in those miserable months after her mother's death.

The smell made her pause at the half-open door of her room. As foul as the air was, she was startled at the scent of tobacco in the air. Because neither her father nor Peter smoked, the smell was one she associated with the drinking bars and gambling houses she walked past downtown.

She paused, her heart suddenly thumping, then peered carefully around the door.

A looter. She was too startled to move. She stared dumbly at the picture of a strange man standing in her room.

His back was to her as he opened and shut the drawers of her dressing table. Just the size of his broad and muscular back under his soiled, blue work shirt scared her. Mrs. Turner's words came back, "women with small children here alone." He was wearing a dark hat with a wide brim and had apparently entered by climbing the roof of the porch, which the wind had driven into her bedroom, leaving a gaping hole.

What if she went away, just backed out and went downstairs and let him loot whatever he could find? Before she could answer her own question, he turned a little, giving her a glimpse of something under his left arm.

Shells. Her shell-trimmed trinket box. How crazy. Why would a looter take the chance of his life for a silly box holding nothing but a young girl's costume jewelry, beads and pins? But he wouldn't know that. He would think it contained *real* jewelry, things of genuine value.

The memory struck her with a gasp. The pearls. She had put her mother's pearls in that box the night of her birthday. Just as the realization struck her, she heard Hildy's plaintive voice calling from the stairs.

"Darcy, where are you? Are you up there, Darcy?"

The broad man's hands stopped moving as he stood very still, waiting.

In a minute he'll look around, Darcy thought with horror. He'll see me and then he'll run away with my mother's pearls. She flattened herself back against the door and looked around desperately. She had no time to think. She needed something she could hurl at him, to startle him into releasing the trinket box. In two swift steps she reached the hall table where Hildy kept a kerosene lamp for nights when the electricity failed. As her hand closed around the lamp, she kicked the door open, pulled her arm back and hurled the lamp as hard as she could toward the huge man who stared at her dumbly with his back against the outside light.

The lamp didn't hit him. Instead it struck an exposed rafter on the wall above his head. The glass shattered and spilled the reeking kerosene down over his head and shirt. He cried out, threw up his hands and flailed for balance.

She heard him fall out of the house, then howl as if in pain.

Hildy was running on the stairs. "Darcy!" she was screaming. "Darcy, what happened? Are you all right?"

"I'm fine," Darcy called. "I'm all right. I'm fine."

She wasn't fine. Her breath wouldn't work and her knees were warm jelly. But the box had flown from his hand to spill the pearls in among the other trinkets on the floor. She scooped up the pearls and turned just as Hildy reached the doorway.

"Darcy," Hildy panted, "what happened? Did you fall?"

"A man," Darcy said. "A man fell."

"What man?" Hildy asked, looking around the room.

"A looter," Darcy gasped. She held out the gleaming strand of pearls with a trembling hand. "I maybe even killed him."

Hildy gaped a moment, then took her arm. "Come downstairs, love. I'll make you hot tea. We need to talk."

She knew it was hysteria but Darcy had the wildest desire to break into laughter. She barely choked it back as Hildy guided her along with a trembling hand. It was for all the world as if Hildy thought that anyone who killed a man should be punished with a hot cup of tea and conversation.

Just as they reached the kitchen, Rose, who had been out in back with the baby, came running into the room breathlessly. "Hildy," she cried. "What in the world is going on? A man just fell off the roof of our house."

"Where is he now?" Hildy asked, whirling on her.

"Running off north," Rose said. "With Buffy hard on his heels."

"Buffy," Darcy cried, rising. "He could hurt Buffy."

Hildy shook her head. "He's not going to stop running for a pint of a dog like that. They *shoot* looters."

"I'm just glad I was out back instead of front," Rose said when Darcy finished her tale. "He could have landed on Sealy and squashed him flat."

Hildy stared at her. "Is that what you've named the little fellow, Sealy?"

Rose shook her head. "You know he had a name before I found him, Hildy. I just *call* him that because I found him on Sealy Street. 'Baby' sounded so impersonal."

Once the tea was brewed, Hildy ordered both of them to sit down. When Hildy then took a chair facing both Darcy and Rose, Darcy's stomach developed a sudden knot. She knew from the expression on the older woman's face that Hildy wasn't planning an ordinary conversation. Darcy held her steaming cup with both hands, waiting.

"We three have to talk," Hildy said heavily. "We need to talk very seriously about what we're going to do."

"We're going to wait for Papa," Darcy put in quickly.

"We're going to *hope* for your papa, and we're going to cling to our faith that he'll be saved, but we have to think what we'll do if he doesn't come home."

Darcy caught a painful breath, but Hildy barked at her. "Don't you start that, young lady. There's a time to plan and a time to weep. This is a planning time."

Rose listened quietly while Hildy repeated Mrs. Turner's bad news about the condition of the city. "And she was right. She was barely out of the house before that looter coming in here made her words sound like gospel. And we're not talking about being away for a long time. This city is picking itself up by its bootstraps fast. I heard the news shouted along the street that the city waterworks had been repaired. That means there'll be some decent water for folks to get this afternoon. Right away they'll have the telegraph fixed and then the telephone. Right away after that there'll be boats passing back and forth from here to the mainland. Your folks are going to come looking for you, Rose. You know they are already half out of their minds."

"The way we are about Uncle Amos," Rose murmured, her eyes on the dozing baby in her lap.

"Darcy will go with your folks, just as they asked."

She glared, stopping Darcy's protest. "Listen to me! Peter and I will hold this place until there's word of the captain, but you, Darcy, are going to Houston with Rose at the first passing." She rose and went to the stove so that her back was turned to Darcy.

"In the meantime, both you girls are going to take shelter in some safer place."

Darcy stared at her in disbelief but Hildy didn't turn to meet her eyes.

"You can't mean that," Darcy cried. "You can't send me off to the Turners. I won't go."

"Darcy Dunlop, are you out to prove that every ugly word that woman said about you is true?" Hildy challenged her.

Darcy put her face in her hands, her arms tight against her chest. Wasn't it enough that the storm had stripped away her father, wrecked her home, destroyed the city and layered it with the stench of death?

She felt Hildy's hand gentle on her shoulder. "Another day," Hildy said softly. "We'll give it at least one more day. And all the faith and hope we can muster."

Chapter Thirteen

DARCY carried both Mrs. Turner's words and Hildy's veiled threat like dead weights all the rest of that Monday. She worked alongside Hildy, not caring that her arms ached and her back felt as if it might crack in two at any moment. Late that afternoon Rose offered to go after water at one of the city's supply depots.

"Tomorrow," Hildy promised, glancing at Darcy. "I don't want you wandering around by yourself with this town still stiff with soldiers and strangers. I'd go with you myself if I weren't so tired. And Darcy's been a little workhorse all day. She's earned some rest."

Darcy *was* tired. Together she and Hildy had made the lower rooms of the house livable. The rugs they had hauled down the uncertain stairway covered the freshly mended holes in the floors. The portrait of her mother was even hanging again above the water-stained mantel of the fireplace. At Hildy's insistence, they had bumped the heavy bed frames downstairs to lift the mattresses off the bare floors. Peter insisted he wanted to stay in the carriage house. A small bed from the old nursery was set up in the dining room for Rose. "This way she and her baby can coo to each other all night without wakening another soul," Hildy explained. Hildy herself had a single bed in the library and Darcy's own bed was set up in the parlor.

Being tired was not the worst part of it. She was disheartened. One more day was all Hildy had promised. At least she would know that Peter, who would stay to guard the house, would be comfortable.

But she didn't even *know* that. Too many things were going on that she didn't know about or understand and there was no one to explain them. No matter which way she looked, she saw fires burning, smudgy fires that fed dark columns of smoke into the sky all day long. Hildy suggested the city was burning away debris. That explanation didn't make very good sense to her. Why would they burn the remains of houses when so much material would be needed for the rebuilding?

Peter came limping home pale and exhausted and reluctant to talk. Darcy felt as cut off from life as the island was cut off from the rest of the world.

When the house finally settled for the night, she

took Buffy out on the porch and sat with her head against a post to watch the moon scatter its light across the water. There was boat traffic on the gulf again. She watched four tugboats pushing a huge barge out toward the horizon line of the gulf. She shut her eyes with pain. What had Mrs. Turner said? "Hundreds, maybe a thousand, souls on a barge to be towed out into the gulf for burial at sea — nameless, unidentified bodies." When she opened her eyes again, the smoke from the reeking, smoldering fires had faded the stars to cold pinpoints of distant light.

Buffy stiffened against her and would have barked if Darcy hadn't caught his muzzle in her hand. She hushed him quietly. Cross at herself for letting Mrs. Turner's dire reports affect her, she deliberatly tightened her body against the post to control her mounting terror. The scrape of footsteps came steadily closer.

For a crazy moment she thought it might be Michael. Then an unfamiliar voice spoke.

"Miss," a man called, his voice rough and guttural, "is there a Peter Hardesty here?"

She hesitated, then nodded. "Yes, he's sleeping."

"I need to speak with him," the man said. "If you'd be so kind."

"Couldn't it wait until tomorrow?" she asked hesitantly, remembering the gray exhaustion in Peter's face.

"I talked with him when he was going through

the morgues today," the man said. "He was looking for a friend."

Darcy leaped to her feet. "Captain Dunlop?" she asked.

"Hold up there," he cautioned. "I've no certainty it's the right man."

"Wait here," she cried, running to waken Peter.

Peter groaned at her touch on his shoulder, but sat up quickly when her message got through to him.

"You wait here," he told her when they reached the front of the house.

"Oh, Peter, no," Darcy pleaded.

"You'll wait here," he repeated with uncharacteristic firmness. "At least until I hear what he has to say."

Peter limped down the walk. The two men, eerily bathed in moonlight, talked only briefly. With the stranger still standing in the shadows, Peter returned. Darcy's heart sank at his expression.

"Tell me," she whispered. "What did he say?"

"That some say it's the captain they found and others aren't sure."

"He's not dead," Darcy cried, seizing his arm.

He shook his head. "The man he speaks of is still alive. He's in a deep coma, neither speaking nor seeming to hear. Him and some others were trapped in a ship's cabin that was crushed by impact. They've been penned up for at least three days without much air and no food and water. Remember, we have no certainty that it's him," he reminded her, raising his voice in warning.

"But if it was the *Sojourner*," she reminded him.

"There wasn't enough left of the ship for a man to tell," Peter told her.

"Oh, Peter," she pleaded. "Let me go with you."

He hesitated. "There's more to the problem than that," he said reluctantly. "If it's our captain, there's the problem of getting him home." His tone turned cross with frustration. "Use your reason, child. If this be the captain and him not conscious to give his name, how could he walk the length of this island?"

Darcy caught a deep breath. They needed a horse and a rig of some kind, even a cart would do. Their own horse, Jemmy, had disappeared in the storm, swept away when the stable tore loose from its foundation. Her heart plunged, remembering the smart rig Mrs. Turner had arrived and departed in. Before she found words, Peter spoke hesitantly.

"What about your friend's pa, the builder Morton? Would he have somewhat we could borrow?"

Mr. Morton. Darcy clapped her hands tightly together. "Oh, thank you, Peter. Thank you," she cried.

Then her heart sank. How could she make herself go back to that house with Angela's words still etched so painfully in her mind? She could only do it for Papa.

"We could try, Peter. Oh, please, let me come along. I have to."

His laugh was brief and without humor. "You'll certainly have to if we're to beg a rig from Morton at such an hour," he said dryly. "Though I would give a pretty penny to save you the trip."

She would have left that moment except for Peter's quick reproach. "You're not aiming to take off without telling Hildy?" he asked in amazement.

Spoiled. Selfish. Thoughtless.

"No," she said swiftly. "Of course not, Peter," she protested, awash with sudden guilt.

Hildy stared at her in the darkness. She had braided her generous gray hair into plaits that rested girlishly on the shoulders of her flannel gown. She sat up at once, her hands trembling as she groped to loosen her hair.

"Stay and rest," Darcy told her.

Hildy glared at her. "Fine lot of rest I'd have with you chasing around in the middle of the night and our not knowing if that poor man is our captain or not!"

Darcy's heart sank to see the Morton house in apparent darkness. She stood hesitant a long moment before getting up enough courage to approach the front door. Peter danced with nervousness in the dark of the porch behind her and the rough-voiced stranger waited at the edge of the street.

Although she rapped with the brass knocker only once and then but lightly, the door opened almost at once. The drapes and the carefully fitted shutters had completely shut in the glow of the kerosene lamp. Its warm, acrid smell filled the foyer. When the light from the doorway fell on her face, Mr. Morton's astonishment was evident in his voice. "Darcy, my child."

He would have drawn her into the light but she protested. "I've come begging," she told him, explaining quickly what her errand was.

He peered at Peter in the darkness, and took her hand. "It's a few minutes of work to hitch a rig," he said. "Wouldn't you be more comfortable inside?"

She shook her head and waited in the dimness of the stable as he and Peter harnessed a sleepy, dappled horse. "It won't be the best riding," Mr. Morton told Darcy, "but a cart seems the best choice."

She nodded, conscious of the minutes spinning by. When Mr. Morton insisted on driving them himself, she protested at once.

"My dear," he said, handing her up onto the seat, "I do no less for you than your father would for my Angela."

She was grateful that the driving demanded his whole attention. Had Angela spilled her wild story to him? And what of Michael? Remembering her last glimpse of him, startled and staring at Angela's door as she flew past, she flushed with embarrassment. She had run away like a fugitive only to come back and beg help from this family. Only for her father, she told herself. She would only have undertaken this imposition on Mr. Morton for her father's sake.

* * *

Following directions from the stranger in the back of the cart, Mr. Morton drove north to the main part of town. The full moon bathed the ruined buildings in an eerie light. The horse's hooves clattered in the quiet streets. The only sound of life came from the footsteps of the soldiers patrolling the empty roads. As they passed these young men, the cart's lantern blinked on the polished metal of their bayonets. She could hardly believe her eyes to see how many of the streets were almost wholly free of rubble.

"It's been a yeoman's job," Mr. Morton nodded at her comment. "The people of Galveston have risen to this like heroes." Then he laughed almost bitterly. "Some have had heroism thrust upon them."

At Darcy's questioning glance, he shook his head. "It's not pretty work or easy, and many want no part of it. The mayor came up with the answer. Work or starve. No food is allowed for anyone who doesn't do their share."

She thought of Michael shielding her against the flying rubbish so recently cleaned from these thoroughfares. She wondered if Mr. Morton knew what she and Michael had been through together that terrible day and night. "Did you realize that Michael saved my life?" she asked. "Not once, but a dozen times during the storm."

He looked over at her and shook his head. "I was

so grateful when he returned that I didn't ask how that came to be. Then you were together all that time?"

Her heart seemed to stop at his words. "Escapade," Mrs. Turner called it.

"We were caught downtown when the wind changed," she explained. "I gave up a dozen times. Michael never did."

He nodded beside her. "He's a rare one, that lad, and the city itself is lucky that the storm caught him here. Many a willing man brings strength but no skill to the task facing us. Michael also has the skill. He's a fine engineer if I do brag on the boy myself."

His words were interrupted by the stranger leaning forward to tap his shoulder. "You'll need to veer right in a few yards," the man warned him.

Mr. Morton obediently turned to drive the cart down a side road. Only a few feet farther, the horse's passage was blocked by debris.

"He says we can walk from here," Peter said, jumping down. He turned to Mr. Morton plaintively. "Could you get Miss Darcy to wait here with the rig?"

"I doubt that very much," Mr. Morton said, catching Darcy under her arms and lifting her down as if she were a child. With Peter carrying the lantern from the cart, Angela's father tucked Darcy's hand in under his arm as they followed the stranger through the cluttered darkness.

Darcy tried not to breathe the air. The smoke of

nearby smoldering fires only worsened the stench that hung over the area. The stranger quickened his steps, turned to the right and bent low to pull back a covering from a lean-to shanty. Peter followed him with the lantern, his body wholly concealing what lay in the makeshift shelter beyond.

Darcy felt her heart thunder. She clung to Mr. Morton's arm for what seemed a silent eternity. Then Peter limped out, holding the lantern high as if it were a triumphant torch. His voice cracked crazily with emotion.

"It's himself," he cried. "Himself in the flesh, the saints be praised." When Darcy pressed toward him, Peter caught her arm and held her back.

"Back to the cart with you," he ordered her with a warning glance at Mr. Morton.

"Indeed," Mr. Morton said hastily. "Peter's right. Back to the cart with you." Giving her no alternative, he hustled her through the rubbish to where the horse waited. Ignoring her protest, he whisked her up onto the seat.

"You're not to follow me," he told her sternly.

Only when she nodded did he turn to join the other men. Her hands ached from gripping themselves as she waited. Why was it taking them so long? The horse stamped impatiently and a night bird flew over very low, its wings swishing in the silence.

The lantern finally emerged from the opening in the shanty. After it came the other two men, bearing her father's silent body on a makeshift wooden stretcher. From the uneven passage of the lantern, she knew that Peter was lighting the way for his companions.

Only after they eased their burden into the cart could she actually see her father's face. He was as pale as death and the bones of his cheeks seemed stronger and sharper. She clambered out of her seat to kneel at his side. The sour stench of decay was so strong around him that she had to touch his flesh to assure herself that he was really alive. The flesh of his cheek was warm to the touch without any suggestion of fever. As she studied him, his eyes rolled under his closed lids and he sighed. Weak with relief and gratitude, she crawled back up into the seat, leaned her head against Mr. Morton's shoulder and wept.

As Mr. Morton turned the cart toward home, she heard the stranger's whispered question to Peter. She stubbornly refused to deal with its implication in her mind.

"And the others. They were strangers to you?" he asked.

"Aye," Peter mumbled. "Strangers. God rest their souls."

Mr. Morton seemed to be thinking out loud. "He belongs in a hospital," he said thoughtfully. Before Darcy could protest, he went on. "Unfortunately there's no question of that, I'm afraid."

"Hildy and I — " Darcy began.

"A doctor needs to see him," Mr. Morton went

on as if she hadn't spoken. "There's an equally poor chance for that tonight, I fear. But I'll see that he gets medical care the first thing come morning."

"If we can just get him home," Darcy said, "I know he'll be better. A hot bath," she chattered. "Something in his stomach. He has no fever."

Mr. Morton glanced down at her, then smiled. "What a mercy that he's been found."

Darcy nodded and blinked back her tears. His own family had not been so lucky. She laid her hand on his arm. "I'll never be able to thank you enough."

"Nor I you," he said quietly, "that you called on me."

When Mr. Morton drew the horse to a stop in front of the house, he looked over at Darcy in horror. "What's this?" he asked, his tone angry. "Look at that porch, that roof! It's not safe for human habitation. Why didn't someone tell me how much damage you had?"

"It's shelter," Peter said.

"Shelter!" Mr. Morton cried. "Use your head, man. We can't take a sick man into that ruin. Darcy, there's room to spare at my place."

Hildy was already down the stairs, leaning into the cart over the captain's body. "Hold up that lantern, Peter," she ordered. "How is he hurt?" Like Darcy, she felt his face for fever.

"Listen, Hildy," Mr. Morton said, down from the cart at her side. "We've a working kitchen at my house and clean, fresh rooms."

"And we've the same," she told him. "At least on the main floor."

Mr. Morton groaned and stared up at the house with a builder's squint. "But the roof, that crushed porch."

"Please, Mr. Morton. I know Papa wants to be home," Darcy pleaded, trying to keep the tears from her voice.

He looked down at her and sighed. "Very well, my dear." His tone was one of resignation. "But you mark my words. I'll have this house looked at tomorrow. If it isn't completely safe for the lot of you, you're coming home with me."

Peter seemed to have forgotten his exhaustion. Once the captain was bathed and laid on the mattress in the parlor, Peter returned to the kitchen, frowning.

"And how badly is he hurt?" Hildy asked.

"He breathes too light. He has a shoulder broke and maybe an arm," Peter said. "Bruises for the length of him, and thin as a wire."

"Why doesn't he waken?" Darcy asked.

Peter shook his head. "There's a lump on his head to the right but no blood flowed." He looked up at Hildy with a thoughtful glance. "When would you say the last food or drink passed his mouth?"

Hildy glanced at Darcy. "Maybe noon on Saturday," Darcy said. It was then she and Michael had seen the ship moored and the cabin locked tight.

"We could try to get something down his throat,"

Darcy suggested. "Maybe a little warm tea."

"Tea!" Hildy scoffed. "What he needs is a rich bowl of broth with egg noodles and chunks of the chicken."

"You women yammer on," Peter said. "The man needs something hot to drink and it's little matter what it be."

When he rose and began to clatter about Hildy's cupboard she followed in protest. He brushed her away, put a generous dollop of honey in a cup and added warmed water.

"Here," he said, handing it to Darcy. "You pour and I'll mop."

With Hildy propping up his head, Darcy carefully leaked the warm liquid between her father's lips. At first it simply flowed down on the towel Peter held beneath his chin. Then, miraculously, he swallowed, coughed, and swallowed again until the cup was empty.

Peter looked up triumphant. "That'll set him on the right course," he said, nodding.

Darcy won the battle of wills. Logic was on her side, but she finally prevailed with tears. Peter and Hildy, both frowning with doubt, went off to bed, leaving Darcy curled in her blankets to serve as night nurse.

Darcy meant not to sleep at all. The labor of the past day overwhelmed her. She dozed lightly, wakening now and then to listen to her father's breathing. Perhaps it was only hope, but she thought it seemed less shallow as the night passed. Once he groaned and shifted. She was instantly at his side but he did not open his eyes or move again. Since there was no going back to sleep, she put her pillow on the windowsill and stared out at the darkness. There, with the night wind cool on her face, she finally slept.

The morning birds wakened her with a start. As she stretched and sat up, she barely stifled a cry. Michael was sitting silently on the top stair of the porch just as she had the evening before, staring off at the dawn just breaking across the gulf.

He sensed her glance and came quietly to kneel on the porch just outside of the window.

"Good morning," he said, his smile no less brilliant for the shadows of fatigue under his eyes.

"Have you been here all night?" she asked in disbelief.

"Not *all* night," he corrected her. "Just since Uncle came home at midnight, stamping and roaring about the condition of this house. I was lucky to get off with my head for not telling him how much damage it had taken."

"You *did* have other things on your mind," Darcy whispered. "How is Angela?"

"Probably as weak as a snail," he said. "She has refused to come out of that room since Auntie's funeral."

Darcy sighed. "Not even for meals?"

Michael smiled a little, apparently knowing Angela's appetite as well as Darcy did. Then he reached for her hand. "Haven't I missed you though, Darcy! Tell me about your father."

She looked at him with the morning light gilding his hair and his eyes warm and intense on her own.

"He's alive, Michael," she said.

He studied her a moment, then lifted her hand and pressed it to his lips. "We know what that means, don't we?" he whispered huskily. "We know."

Behind her, Darcy heard Hildy moving about in the kitchen. Darcy and Michael both rose, but he did not release her hand for a long moment.

"I leave you with three pieces of important information," he said in a very official tone. "The barometer is rising, promising fair weather ahead. I'll be back before evening with a crew to see what can be done about this house."

Then his eyes crinkled with laughter. "This last announcement is the most important. I love you."

He was still laughing softly as he leaped off the porch and went across the yard in a swinging gait. He didn't look back at all but only did a little cakewalk as he passed the stub of the palm tree where he had first kissed her.

Chapter Fourteen

THE doctor Mr. Morton had contacted arrived before Hildy got her hair out of braids. He rapped on the broken door with the head of an ebony cane, then stuck his head in through the broken porch window.

Darcy, who had come flying in from the kitchen, stared at him in astonishment.

"I'm presuming my welcome," he said, climbing into the room. He set his hat on the table and offered Darcy a hand whose grip was remarkably cool and strong. Even as he spoke, his eyes, behind gold wire-rimmed glasses, studied the man on the bed. He took off his coat and handed it to Darcy, and began to roll up the sleeves of his shirt.

Then he looked at her and sniffed the air with an expression of wonder. "How can it possibly smell good in here?" he asked, drawing a deep breath.

"Spices," Darcy explained. "Hildy cooks them in a spirit lamp."

"She's a genius," he said. As he spoke, Hildy, her hair bundled around her head, appeared in the door.

"Ah," the doctor said, smiling at her. "The genius of the spirit lamp. Hildy, I will need a man of some strength to help me. This great giant here has bones that need setting."

"Yes, sir," she said, starting to back out the door.

"No," he said. "Send this lovely child for help. I need to talk to you."

Darcy started for the carriage house without being told. When she called up to Peter that the doctor had come, he came swinging down the ladder like a youngster smiling with delight.

"It's only a matter of time now, Miss," he told Darcy as he shot by her. "Only a matter of time."

In the few minutes she had been gone, the house had become a beehive of industry. Hildy had fed the wood range with half-dried wood that crackled as it caught ablaze. The doctor, his instruments on a fresh towel beside her father's bed, bent with his stethoscope on the captain's chest, and his eyes on his watch.

He nodded a greeting to Peter, then turned to Hildy. "One thing before we start. Is there somewhere you can send the children? And the baby?" He frowned in a puzzled way at Rose, who had come to the doorway with Sealy nestled against her shoulder. "Out in back," he added hastily. "Under no circumstances must they even look toward the beach."

When Darcy stared at him, he shook his head. "You are not to go anywhere today where you can even *see* the beach," he said firmly. Then he added more gently, "Those are doctor's orders."

"The carriage house," Hildy said, giving Rose a nudge. "We'll come for you when we can."

It was Peter who came for them. He was smiling but his shirt, around the collar and all down the front, was darkened with sweat as if he had been doing heavy labor.

"How is he?" Darcy asked.

Peter grinned broadly. "The man that he is and always has been."

"Where is all that shoveling noise coming from?" Darcy asked him as she took Sealy from Rose's arms so her cousin could climb down behind her.

"The beach," he growled, turning away to start back to the house.

Darcy's father lay with his head back, as if exhausted. It took a minute to realize that his odd posture was due to bindings around his right shoulder and a cast fastened to his arm.

"How is he?" she whispered to the doctor.

"Ask him," he said in a light, almost merry tone of voice.

Darcy leaned over the bed. "Papa?" she whispered.

He opened his eyes slowly and smiled, reaching for her with his good hand.

"Dreaming," he said weakly. "If I didn't know better, I'd say it was my sweet sixteen-year-old daughter." He paused, his hand on hers. "And Rose?"

"Right here, Uncle Amos," she lilted, starting toward him.

"Careful, love," he said in a warning tone.

"Rose is changed, Captain," Hildy said. "She hasn't even broken a dish since the storm."

Darcy looked at Hildy in amazement. It was true, Rose hadn't stumbled, or dropped anything or even been awkward for a moment.

"I have to be careful because of Sealy," she explained.

The captain only smiled, and his eyelids drooped shut. The doctor took Darcy's hand and motioned them all toward the kitchen. Once there, he explained. "He'll have little spurts of energy like that for a few days, then will sleep for hours. But once his strength begins to come back, he'll be himself again. I've gone through his nursing needs with Hildy and I'll deal with Morton for you."

"Morton?" Darcy asked, confused.

"He gave me orders to tend your father, then have him moved over to the Morton house. He can't be moved without risk. Hildy assures me you can care for him here."

"Oh, we can. We can," Darcy cried, scarcely restraining herself from hugging this wry, cheerful man who had come as a stranger only an hour or so before.

He smiled and turned to Rose. "Now let me take a look at that baby."

Rose nodded. It took a moment for the doctor to coax the child from Rose's arms, then he tickled the boy's tummy and bounced him playfully, studying his face.

"Why is it that you call him Sealy?" he asked quietly. "Is that where you found him?"

Peter answered for her, his voice low and gruff. "He alone survived in a crushed house on that street."

The doctor nodded and handed the baby back to Rose. "I thought I recognized him. I brought this fine fellow into the world. His real name is Andrew and you've taken wonderful care of him."

Rose studied his face silently, waiting.

"He's among the lucky ones," the doctor said. His expression was strange, almost apprehensive as he watched Rose's face. "There must be a thousand orphans in this city since the storm. First, he had you to care for him. Then, when there's passing, he has a young grandmother who adores him in Texas City."

Darcy caught her breath, terrified of Rose's reaction. Watching Rose cuddle the child, care for him, and play with him, she had shuddered to think how it would all end. Even if this little boy had been orphaned by the storm, he couldn't be just handed over to a fifteen-year-old girl as if he were an entrancing toy. Even in this unlikely event, what would her Aunt Julie say if she came for one child and found herself with two? Now those problems were wiped away only to be replaced by another. No wonder the doctor had looked apprehensive. How was this strange, merry little girl going to react to losing the child that she had loved so tenderly the past days? At Rose's smile, Darcy let her breath out slowly.

She had woefully underestimated her cousin. Rose beamed with delight. "Oh, thank you, thank you!" she told the doctor. "I was so afraid, so afraid — " Darcy realized that only the squirming baby kept Rose from throwing her arms around the man.

Hildy's eyes swam with tears. "What would you like, Doctor? Tea, a cup of coffee, maybe a bite to eat?" she asked. "What can we do for you until you're better paid?"

"Nothing," he began, then paused. "There *is* something. Tell me how you've driven the smell of death from this house."

Hildy whirled to the cupboard and folded a generous collection of the spices into a paper to hand to him. "Cinnamon, nutmeg, and bay leaf," she told him. "And the rind of orange would add a lot if you had some."

Having the captain there to care for, being able

to look in the doorway and see him peacefully sleeping, changed the whole world for Darcy. She and Rose carried buckets and brought back sweet city water for tea and coffee. To Darcy's amazement, the *Galveston News* was being sold on the street. She bought a copy for Hildy and tucked it under her belt to leave both her hands free.

The water was so heavy that they moved slowly, now and then stopping for breath and to rest a minute. Fires still smoldered around the city. In every block they passed, men labored with shovels and levers, searching the debris.

"When do you think my parents can get here?" Rose asked a little wistfully.

"Any day now," Darcy assured her. "By now the whole country must know what's happened to Galveston."

"But you heard what that woman said," Rose reminded her. "That the mayor had sent appeals for help and asked that nobody come here."

"He meant that for idlers and curiosity seekers," Darcy told her.

Rose shook her head. "She said he was even telling people not to come check on their families, and for everyone here who could, to leave."

Darcy stumbled a little, sloshing water on her skirt. All day she had gone from one joy to another and back. Having her father safe and mending was the first great joy, but there was also Michael. He had promised to come back "with a crew of men."

Since he hadn't said when, she suddenly wanted to hurry back home. Would he be sent away with the others who didn't belong on the island, the visitors like Rose, and the tourists who had been caught there?

Michael and his crew arrived a little after four. As the other three men circled the house, eyeing the damages and talking quietly to each other, Michael came to the porch window.

Seeing the captain there, he flushed and took off his cap.

"Welcome home, sir," he said as the captain stared at his sudden appearance at the window.

Darcy's father nodded and said, "Come in, Michael. Is there something wrong with the door?"

"Oh, no, sir," Michael said, grinning at Darcy and stepping in over the sill. "The door is fine. We just can't use it until the porch roof is taken off it."

The captain stared at him and then began to shake under his light sheet. "Stop that, young man," he said. "You can't imagine how much it hurts to laugh."

Darcy pulled a chair from against the wall, helpless with delight. Her father had smiled. He had eaten and drunk and slept but he had not jiggled with laughter, nor even looked as if he were about to until that moment.

"I can't imagine why I'm laughing," Darcy's father admitted. "How bad is the damage?"

"We're checking that right now. Uncle says that this house was so well built that it can probably be made habitable in a few days."

The captain fell silent. "I feel bad about Morton's men coming here. There must be many houses in worse shape than this one."

"Hundreds," Michael said cheerfully. "Nearly four thousand houses were completely blown away."

The captain stared at him. "Four thousand," he whispered. "And the loss of life?"

Michael glanced at Darcy, then away. His humor gone, his voice fell. "They are guessing nearly six thousand," he said.

The captain reached for Darcy with his good arm, not needing to say what was on his mind.

"Papa," Darcy began, meaning to tell her father what role Michael played in her survival. But Michael would have none of it.

"Beg your pardon, sir," Michael said brusquely. "I need your go-ahead on the temporary repair of your house."

"Oh, you have it, you have it," the captain said. "But is Morton sure he wants to do this when so many others need help?"

"Oh. Perfectly sure," Michael said, rising and winking at Darcy. "He's afraid that, otherwise, you'd have to dynamite this place to get your daughter out."

When the captain looked at Darcy, she flushed

and shrugged. "I didn't mean to leave until you came home, that was all."

Michael and his crew worked steadily all afternoon. They lifted the porch roof off and laid it in the yard. They had begun repairs on the gaping hole the roof had left in the wall of Darcy's bedroom when the last vestiges of light left the sky.

Then Michael came to the door and knocked quite formally. Darcy opened it, laughing, since he had just let the workmen out through the same door.

"Good evening, Miss Dunlop," he said formally. "Would you care to take a constitutional with me?"

Then she really laughed. Only the stiffest of the old people she knew still called a walk "a constitutional."

"I'll have to ask Papa," she said primly.

"For heaven's sake go with him," her father called from the next room. "I can take any punishment but his jokes."

"The beach is out of bounds," Michael said as he led her around the house. She nodded. She had been curious about the doctor's orders to her and Rose that they must not even look at the beach. Later, when she read the paper, she wished she hadn't learned what he was protecting them from. Most of the seven hundred bodies towed out for sea burial had returned with the morning tide. All that day they had been burning the corpses or burying them where they lay.

They walked in silence a little while. When Michael took her hand, she didn't pull hers away.

"Michael," she finally said.

"Wait," he interrupted her. "Let's make a rule that we only talk of happy things, silly things if you will, things that make us laugh. We don't have enough time to waste any, Darcy."

His words were like a blow. Why did he have to remind her that he would be leaving? As if she could forget it.

"I don't know how we can do that," she admitted.

He turned to her suddenly. "By trying very hard. Nothing we can do can take away the horror around us. Nothing we can say, over and over, can make us forget it. Clinging to all the life we have is the only way to go."

She nodded but was silent.

"You can't think of anything happy?" he asked her.

"Oh, yes," she admitted. "Finding Papa was like a miracle. And did I tell you about Rose's baby?"

He stopped dead still. "Rose's *what?*"

"Hush, you're shouting," she said. Then she realized he had left before Rose came home. He had only been there with her father and herself when Rose was off with Sealy and Hildy.

She didn't exaggerate much but she did make as good a story of it as she could. She described Rose's arrival with a sputtering Peter and this sturdy infant wrapped in her petticoat. She told of how Peter had hung tea towels to dry on the stripped branches of once flowering bushes because there hadn't been a diaper in the house since Darcy herself was a baby.

In the end, as they turned back toward the house, they were both laughing. Before they reached the light streaming from the lamp beside her father's bed, Michael stopped her in the shadows.

"Darcy, you are the most entertaining girl I have ever met in my life. I'm sorry we're not *really* engaged so I could look forward to enjoying you forever! No wonder my cousin Angie loves you so much."

She winced at the sudden stab of pain.

"What's wrong?" he asked.

"I'm not sure she does anymore," she whispered.

"Of course she does. She was crazy as a loon those first few days after losing Auntie. I didn't blame her; they were really close. Then she healed, just like your dad is doing. This morning when I came back from here she wanted to know all about you and Hildy and Rose. Wait'll I tell her about Rose's baby!"

"You're sure, Michael?"

"Certain," he said. "She wanted to send you something today. She went through the cupboards like a madwoman. She was looking for chocolates because she said you loved them."

"Oh, Michael," she sighed.

"I didn't bring you anything," he told her. "The only thing she found to send you was salt-water taffy."

She stared at him in the darkness and began to

laugh. He caught her and silenced her with a swift, gentle kiss.

"You know that I love you, don't you?" he whispered.

She nodded and fought back tears.

Chapter Fifteen

ALL of her life Darcy had *thought* she understood hurricanes. These great storms started hundreds of miles away in distant waters, whirling in great counterclockwise circles over the face of the seas. Sometimes a storm's strength abated before it reached land. A hurricane was like a spiral cone of wind spinning around its murderous center, known as the eye. When such a storm ventured over land, it battered the area with the highest winds and the greatest power known in the natural world. Between the coming of the storm and its most terrible violence, a treacherous calm prevailed under the eye of the storm. When the storm had spent its fury, the force that had driven the sea onto the land weakened, permitting the storm, like a greedy monster returning to some deep lair, to take with it all the booty it could carry.

Darcy saw the rescue and return of her father as the eye of her personal storm.

Once he was settled safely into the parlor bed, the household fell into a comfortable and peaceful rhythm. Peter still left every morning to put his shoulder to the gigantic task of cleaning up the city. The captain's strength gradually returned, along with a better humor than Darcy remembered his having had before the storm. For one thing, he was entertained during his forced idleness. When Sealy wasn't sleeping or being fed, Rose placed him on a pallet near her uncle. Buffy, who considered the child his responsibility, spent his days in the parlor, watching the child. He even occasionally let the crowing youngster tug his ears and try to catch his stiff, short tail.

But Darcy credited the greater part of her father's geniality to Michael. He and his crew arrived each morning and punctuated the days with hammering and sawing as they restored the Dunlop house. Even with the front door repaired, Michael, like a mischievous boy, stuck his head into the window of the parlor to banter with the captain off and on all day.

"What good company that young man is," the captain told Darcy. "I know Morton is delighted to have him coming on board in his business."

Darcy didn't reply. Michael's decision had been safe with her but it had also been torture. Who knew better than she what good company Michael was? And she clung to that pleasure feverishly, knowing it was winding down like a clock. She loved it that Hildy insisted Michael join her and her father for lunch each day, and when the workmen left he and Darcy had a precious hour alone.

The beaches were finally cleared. Adjutant General Scurry had arrived that night after her father was found and had assumed the authority for martial law. Although his guards were posted along the beaches to keep undesirables from coming onto the island, the beach itself seemed healed. The dolphins were back, cavorting in the rippling water, and seashells studded the white sand.

Although the mayor ordered flour mills and wholesale grocers to hold food supplies for community distribution, one of the grocers, Pabst and Lenbach, opened for business on Wednesday. Hildy was giddy with delight to get a single scrawny chicken to make soup for her patient.

That same day the first mail arrived at the post office. Since there were no deliveries, Darcy went with Rose to wait in line for the mail. Rose clutched the letter from her parents with both hands, pressing it against her chest. She had it open and was reading it before they got out on the street.

"Oh, Darcy," she cried. "Listen to what Mother writes:

" 'Our Houston paper has been carrying interviews with all the people they can find who have escaped Galveston. One of these men, a ship's captain, reported that he heard the Dunlop family, including a visiting niece, had all survived without harm except for Captain Dunlop, whose ship, the *Sojourner*, was found in pieces near Cedar Point. I grieve painfully for the loss of that wonderful man but am holding faith he may yet be found.

" 'As for you, my dear, we will come as soon as permitted. We read the constant pleas by the mayor there for people to leave the island and make new lives elsewhere. We understand many families have already done so. We trust that Darcy and Hildy are preparing to return to Houston with us, and dear Amos, too, if our faith is rewarded by fact. We will be talking to you or seeing you as quickly as possible.' "

Rose looked up at Darcy with tears in her eyes. "Oh, I miss them," she said. "But how glorious it will be when they discover that Uncle Amos is alive and — almost well."

Darcy forced herself to smile back at Rose. Her father apparently had not seen past his recovery to plans for his future. He was not young. He had lost his ship and his business with it. Would he decide to leave the shattered island and begin a new life? She couldn't imagine it. He was a seafaring man. What would he do in a landlocked city like Houston? More than that, he was a Galvestonian. And so was she.

"Have you thought yet about coming home with me?" Rose asked quietly.

Darcy looked at Rose's pretty, fair face. Her shining blue eyes no longer held the openness of innocence. How much she had grown up in this past week. She was as self-contained a girl as one could ask, and her question was tactful and delicately put, nothing like the outbursts of the old Rose.

"I *have* thought," Darcy admitted. "As much as I love you and Aunt Julie, I will only leave Papa if he insists on it. Papa and I are a family, Rose, and both of us belong on this island."

There was more to her decision than she could tell Rose. If it had not been for her father, she would have yearned desperately to be gone away from here — anywhere away. Once Michael left, she would be desolate. Angela sent messages and had even written a couple of loving notes, but Darcy knew their friendship could not survive the past week without being changed. She had had enough of things changed. Michael had said he had messed things up between her and Alex Turner. It was more than that. No matter how much she liked Alex as a person, no matter how gallant and sometimes even entertaining he could be when he wanted to, she would never be able to face him again without the memory of his mother's words scalding her mind.

They walked in silence a few minutes before Rose took her hand. "I *do* understand," she said finally.

Although many of his friends stopped by to visit Darcy's father, he depended on Michael for his news.

"The first water started through the mains today," Michael told him. "I tell you, this city is a wonder. Tomorrow they expect the telegraph to go into operation. I can't imagine another place where everyone would work together like this. Galveston is unique."

"A paradise poised at the gates of destruction," Darcy said quietly.

Her father's head came up sharply and he stared at her. "Darcy!"

Michael said, "That's my fault, sir. She's only quoting me."

"That's how you see our island?" the captain asked, his tone suddenly chilly.

"As it lies," Michael admitted. "But it could be made safe, as I told Darcy."

When her father looked a question at Michael, Darcy excused herself. Now he was going to launch into that talk about the seawall and maybe even tell her father about raising the island above the level of the high tide. She was better off giving Hildy a hand in the kitchen with the evening meal.

Late on Thursday afternoon the telegraph was in operation.

"Tomorrow you must send a great message to your parents," Darcy's father told Rose. "A thousand worried relatives will be relieved to get word from this place."

Rose nodded. "Do you suppose your doctor knows how to reach Sealy's grandmother?" she asked softly.

He nodded. "Talk to Michael about that. He and Mr. Morton would probably be happy to get it for you. We're all going to miss that little scamp, you know."

Rose nodded again. "I'll never forget him." She looked up suddenly. "Do you suppose his grandmother would mind if I kept in touch, even saw him once in a while?"

Darcy's father laughed uproariously. "I'll wager his grandmother will want to give you the moon and seven stars when she has that boy in her arms again — much less an occasional visit."

On Friday, Michael stopped by the kitchen before mounting to the roof, where his crew was already setting out shingling tools. Darcy groaned when he rapped at the door. He never *ever* seemed to catch her any way but disgraceful! She had come down early in a white duster that she only kept to do dirty jobs in. It was cut like a child's smock, making her look all of ten years old and at least two yards around the middle. It didn't help that she had only drawn her hair back with a ribbon and let it fall down her back.

"I came to warn you," he told Darcy. "You've a caller coming today."

She waited, puzzled.

"I thought Uncle was going to choke on his coffee this morning. Angela, who hasn't left the house since Auntie died, announced at breakfast that she was coming to call on you today."

Darcy clasped her hands, wordless with relief and delight.

"It's been a week since your birthday," he reminded her. Then he grinned and looked slyly at Hildy. "I have to warn you that Angie is bringing some little cakes to the captain. Let him eat them at his own risk. She made them herself."

While Hildy launched into Michael for running down Angela's cooking, Darcy stood stunned. Was it possible that only a week had passed since her birthday? How long it seemed since silly things like dance programs had been the most important thing in her life. Only a week ago Michael had kissed her for the very first time and told her he loved her. She looked over at him, feeling a flush of color rise to her cheeks.

He was smiling at her in that warm, gentle way.

"Darcy Dunlop," he said thoughtfully. "You are going to be the most beautiful bride in the history of the world."

Hildy whirled, her eyes wide. "Now what is *that* supposed to mean, young man?" she challenged him.

He shrugged, his eyes wide with mock innocence. "That she looks absolutely wonderful when she wears white, Hildy. What else could I possibly mean?"

He was out the door without waiting for an answer. Hildy shook her head and smiled. "What a tease he is! That young rascal is too much."

Darcy nodded. As long as Michael was here, she

would live more intensely than she ever had in her life. With his going, even her dreams would end.

Angela arrived a little after ten looking so lady-like and proper that Darcy was newly grateful for Michael's warning. At least she had put on a corset and a fresh dress and gotten her hair up. Angela also looked thinner and somehow dimmer than Darcy had ever seen her. The high rosy color was gone from her cheeks and her eyes didn't shine in the old way.

"Gloves!" Darcy exclaimed, still holding Angela's hands after hugging her tight. Angela's mother had waged hopeless campaigns to get her daughter interested in clothes. Failing in that, she had finally settled for getting Angela to wear the things she chose except for gloves and hats, which Angela hated.

Angie grinned with embarrassment. "This is my second try at getting dressed. After I had my cycling clothes on, I remembered that I had another appointment after I leave here. I think I've forgotten how to dress anyway." She glanced down at herself in a worried way. "Does everything match? Do I look all right?"

"Of course you do," Darcy assured her. "Come in and see Papa. He'll be delighted to see you."

He *was* delighted and Angela made instant friends with Rose's baby. "This must be Andrew-called-Sealy, or Sealy-called-Andrew, however you say it."

The captain laughed. "Mostly I just call him, 'Hey, baby' and tell him to quit pulling poor Buffy's ears."

As he spoke, the baby seized Angela's finger and shoved it in his mouth.

"Ouch!" Angela said in astonishment, bringing Rose running. "That little rascal bit me."

"But he hasn't any teeth," Rose protested.

"Now he does," Angela said, exhibiting her finger with a bright red dent in it.

Contrary to what Michael had said, the captain found Angela's homemade cakes delicious and seemed genuinely sorry when Angela rose and said she must go. Darcy walked arm-in-arm with her out to the sidewalk.

"We were walking this way only a week ago," Angela said thoughtfully. Then she sighed and looked tearfully at Darcy.

"Help me, will you, Darcy? Papa is strong and Michael is reasonable. I am neither of those. I just miss my mother so painfully."

Darcy held her close. "You know I'll do all I can," she whispered, fishing for her handkerchief. "Here, wipe your eyes. And let's not go so long without seeing each other again."

Angela nodded and set off with her head high. Her mother would be proud of her, Darcy thought, and fought tears herself.

Every day brought new success in the city's battle against its disaster. On Saturday the streets were clear enough for vehicles to get through and the first streetcar ran. It was car number sixty-six, drawn by a mule named "Lazy Lil." On the excuse of wanting Sealy to see it, Rose walked over to cheer its passing. Sealy slept on her shoulder through the whole event but Rose was heartsick for poor Lil, who dropped from exhaustion after only three round trips.

That same night the first houses glowed with electric lights, but the diggers continued to find dead victims buried under the ruins.

On Sunday, Darcy's father stood on his feet for the first time and took a few hobbling steps, leaning on Peter's shoulders. On the very next day, Clara Barton arrived in Galveston with her staff.

"Clara Barton herself?" the captain asked in amazement.

"In the flesh," Michael reported.

"But she must be a thousand years old!"

"Papa!" Darcy cried. "Now who's exaggerating?"

"I've spent too much time around the two of you," he said. "But I've heard about Clarissa Barton all *my* life. My mother idolized her. She was a schoolteacher for years before she became a nurse during the Civil War, and founded the American Red Cross ages ago. How old is she anyway?"

"Uncle says she's seventy-nine, but you sure wouldn't know it," Michael said. "She's set up headquarters in a tent, but they plan to find her a building right away. Meanwhile she's issuing orders, announcing complicated plans, and serving soup and coffee to the destitute as if she were twenty-nine."

"It does give an old man of thirty-eight some food for thought," the captain said. "She makes it sound as if I have time to start over by having a new ship built."

Darcy caught her breath. He hadn't mentioned the future before at all, much less building a new ship.

"I'm surprised you haven't made plans already," Michael said.

"I've been turning it this way and that in my mind," Darcy's father admitted. "It's hard to decide whether to stay with sails or go with a steamship. Steam *is* the wave of the future." He shook his head. "It's just hard to admit that the great age of sails is past."

"Will this be a *Sojourner II*?" Darcy asked.

"I *have* decided about that," he told her. "It'll be *Yo Solo* this time."

At Michael's confused look, Darcy translated. "That's the motto of the city of Galveston. It means 'I alone.' "

The captain's strength grew daily. On Wednesday he was strong enough to walk with Michael around the house and study the crew's handiwork. "The roof is temporary," Michael told him. "Only adequate to keep out rain." He went on with counsel as to what further work would need to be done when material was available and labor easier to come by.

"I owe you and your uncle more than money can pay," Darcy's father said.

Michael laughed. "You're looking at an engineer playing at being a builder. This is my uncle's doing; he's the one to thank."

"I can't thank him for your good company, son," the captain added. "It's going to be pretty dull around here without your smart remarks."

Darcy felt Michael's eyes on her and glanced up at him.

"I mean to hang around as long as I possibly can," he told her father.

Late in the afternoon on Thursday, a brisk rap sounded at the front door. Darcy, playing cards with Michael and her father in the parlor, started to rise. Since Hildy was passing through the hall, she called out that she would get it.

The conversation was too muffled to understand, but within minutes, Hildy, her face flushed, came to the parlor door accompanied by a trimly dressed stranger.

"She wants to speak to the woman of the house," Hildy said, making no attempt to hide her annoyance.

Startled, Darcy caught her father's nod and rose with all the dignity she could muster.

The woman identified herself crisply. She was working with Clarissa Barton of the American Red Cross in a canvas of the city to locate orphans of the storm. Her eyes flicked with confusion between Darcy and her father as she explained that the Red Cross would take responsibility for such lost children and make every effort to provide them with custodial care. The question, of course, was whether they had an orphaned child needing to be tallied.

Darcy shook her head. "No, we don't."

"You are certain?" the woman pressed.

"Absolutely," Darcy said.

"Is there a child in this house?"

When Darcy hesitated, her father spoke up. "That depends on how you classify a child," he said.

The woman was clearly more uncomfortable with each passing moment. This didn't diminish her persistence. "The child I am seeking is very young, under a year. Have you an orphan child of that age in this household?"

When Darcy shook her head, the woman's tone turned brusque. "Given the circumstances, are you absolutely sure?"

"Madame," the captain asked quietly, "have you reason to challenge my daughter's veracity?"

"No," the woman said. Then she coughed a little. "I mean yes. It's not that I doubt her veracity. It's simply that one of our volunteers particularly mentioned this household as one in which an orphaned child was being housed who might be hidden from the authorities and therefore not included in the census."

Michael, who had stood up immediately when the two women entered, spoke quietly. None of his Yankee rudeness here. As he spoke, he smiled, flowing charm like honey from a hot biscuit. "Perhaps it would be helpful if we knew what volunteer had offered this information."

The woman, eased by his tone, glanced down at her paper. "The name is Turner, Mrs. E. A. Turner. The child is described as being a red-haired boy," she went on, as if to support her insistence with details. "A child of between four and six months of age."

"Ah," Michael said with the merest suggestion of a bow, and a bland smile at Darcy and the captain. "For heaven's sake. She must be talking about Andrew. If you will excuse me, perhaps I can be helpful." He left and ran swiftly up the stairs.

Hildy's face was literally swelling with anger. The captain stared thoughtfully at the doorway Michael had disappeared through. Darcy herself, stunned by Michael's intervention, tried frantically to figure out what he was up to. Where could he have gone except to Darcy's old nursery that Rose and Sealy had shared since the repair of the roof? She did not have to wait long to find out.

The three of them entered together, Michael carrying a brown envelope and Rose, her fair hair loose around her face, bearing the beaming baby.

Sealy smiled at the stranger and reached for her with a chubby fist. "What a lovely child," the woman said, leaning toward him.

"He bites," the captain said unexpectedly from the bed.

Michael, all business, crossed the room to hand the envelope to Darcy. Darcy's fingers trembled as she drew out the papers.

Her knees literally went weak with relief when she realized what Michael had brought her. What was *wrong* with her? She had been with Rose when her cousin sent the first telegraph. The top document was a duplicate of Rose's telegraph message sent to the grandmother's address in Texas City. The second was the grandmother's grateful telegraph in reply. The third was a letter to Rose from the grandmother, telling of her plans to arrive for Andrew on the first train that passed. Her thanks to Rose were effusive and included the doctor's testimony to the heroism with which Rose had dug through rubble to save the child, and her subsequent capable care of him.

Darcy handed the papers to the woman. She read them silently, one after the other. When she looked up, her face was soft with remorse. "Oh, my dear," she said to Rose, then she turned to Darcy. "Do forgive my manner earlier — I had been led to expect — "

"You were misled," Michael said to her gently.

"I was," she agreed, nodding. "Terribly misled. How can I tell you how sorry I am to have been so brusque?" Her eyes were sincere on Darcy's. "We are trying so hard to care for the helpless and needy. But I just simply can't imagine how this happened."

"I have no trouble with that," Hildy said, holding her head at a strange, angry angle. "There are still those among us with nothing better to do than try to make trouble for other people."

The woman looked at her, startled, then nodded as she moved toward the door.

The captain's eyes narrowed as he stared at Michael. "How did you ever manage to put that little plot together?"

"Rose told me about the telegraphs and had shown me the letter. While that woman was talking I remembered Angela coming home exhausted from lunch with that Turner woman last Friday. Angie was as cross as she was angry. She said Mrs. Turner did nothing but ask questions about me and Darcy and Rose and Rose's baby. It just made sense."

"That woman," the captain shook his head. "She's a disgrace to her gender."

"Papa," Darcy said, staring at him. "She gave me to believe that she and Mother were best of friends."

"I'm sure she's perfectly sincere. Your mother *was* nice to her, as nice as she knew how to be," he said, a little huffily. "Your mother wasn't stupid. She always said that Minnie Turner had a tongue like a whipsaw and didn't want her own head cut off."

Michael began to laugh and Sealy, who had just learned to clap, applauded with his sticky hands. Darcy didn't laugh, and neither did Hildy. Darcy saw her own despair matched in Hildy's face.

Chapter Sixteen

DARCY didn't have to read the paper to know what was going on. Between her father and Michael she heard nothing but glowing recitals of the marvelous progress Galveston had achieved in its first thirteen days. On Friday, September the twenty-first, martial law was officially removed even though the militia would remain to keep order as long as was needed.

As soon as the first news of the extent of the hurricane reached the mainland, help began to arrive. Since that day, supply boats had steadily plied the stretch of bay between Texas and Galveston Island, bearing food, medical supplies, and trained personnel to the ruined city. Millions of dollars worth of help had come from everywhere — the federal government, private citizens and other American cities who remembered tragedies of their own. Youngstown, Ohio, still staggering to its feet from its flood; Chicago, whose tragic fire still lingered in its memory. On their return trips the boats carried many individuals and families who were abandoning the island, pledging never to return. But for nearly two weeks the only access to Galveston had been by water.

That Friday brought this isolation to an end. A railroad bridge across the bay had been built in an astonishing five days. It was finished at three o'clock that Friday morning and a Santa Fe train puffed into the station at six twenty that evening.

Since so many people were frantic to reach the city and get news of their families, tickets were hard to obtain. Rose's mother wired she would be there on Tuesday, but Sealy's grandmother arrived the next day.

Darcy studied the woman with relief. It would have been very hard to hand the child they had all learned to love to less than a wonderful person. But she *was* wonderful, a young grandmother as the doctor had said, looking little older than a woman of thirty. She was not only trim and stylish with a great mass of rich auburn hair and a sweet tender smile, but she was thoughtful, too. After struggling for words to thank Rose for saving the child, she knelt beside the baby, who stared at her soberly from Rose's lap.

He did not pull away when she spoke softly to him, but neither did he smile.

"He likes fingers," the captain commented from his invalid chair. The woman gave him a startled smile and waggled her finger at Sealy.

He stared at it cross-eyed for a moment, seized it with both hands and popped it into his mouth.

Her cry of pained astonishment died in her throat as Sealy released her finger and held out his arms to her.

"You didn't tell me he liked to *eat* fingers," she told the captain with a grin, catching Sealy's hand just as he gripped the edge of her hat.

Rose might have been the age of Sealy's grandmother for the dignity she maintained that afternoon. Hildy served tea with spice cakes she had made with the last of the flour. When it was time for them to part, Sealy's grandmother got to her feet. "I had a little speech all in my mind," she admitted. "But it was a speech for strangers." Suddenly her eyes were filled with tears. "You will never be strangers to me, any of you. I did bring my own special treasure as a gift for you, Rose. No, take it," she insisted when Rose protested that she didn't want anything.

Rose opened the velvet box. A gold engraved locket, very tiny and in the shape of a heart, lay against the gray velvet. She tightened her lips and shook her head. "You must not give this to me," she said. "It's wrong."

"No, my dear," the woman said, lifting the locket and prying it open with her fingernail. Sealy's face smiled back at Rose, a younger Sealy but with the same crooked smile. "It would be wrong for me to keep it when I only have him because of you."

The moon that had been full the morning after the storm was altogether gone. A new moon, as slender as the shadow of a smile, hung over the gulf. That night Darcy and Michael walked along the beach in silence. Michael had insisted that they not dwell on unhappy things during their private times together. She had managed pretty well up until this night. Suddenly it was harder.

"Growing old is making you very quiet," he teased.

She laughed and tightened her hand on his arm. He wouldn't want to hear what was in her mind. Sealy was gone. When she left the house Rose had been up in her room carefully folding and packing her clothes to be ready when her own mother arrived to take her home. Within days Rose too would be gone. And it was only a matter of time now before Michael himself would be leaving Galveston to make a new life in the east. The eye of the storm had passed. Now the storm's retreat was carrying everything away. She felt a growing panic about the time to come.

"Has your father made a decision about your going back to Houston with Rose?" he asked.

She looked at him, startled. "How did you know about that?"

"From Angie," he said. "And then your father and I talked about it."

"I'm not really sure I like being discussed behind my back," she told him.

"We love you. How can we help caring?" he said simply.

There was no answer to that. "What do *you* think I should do?" she asked.

He hesitated. "There isn't a school left standing in this city," he said, "and education is very important."

"Michael," she rebuked him. "Save your reports on the progress of the city for Papa. What do you *really* think I should do?"

He turned and took both her hands. "I think you should do whatever will make you happy, Darcy. Nothing in the world matters more than that to me."

"Michael, Michael," she said, suddenly too close to tears to talk. Didn't he realize how much of her happiness depended on him?

"Darcy, Darcy," he mimicked her, with that wonderful twinkle he knew she couldn't resist. "Give me your arm. We'd better go back before Hildy comes after us with fire in her eyes."

As they neared the house, Michael stopped. "I believe your father is entertaining guests."

Darcy followed his eyes and felt herself wilt.

"Mrs. Turner and son?" Michael asked. "Or am I wrong about that fancy rig?"

She shook her head. "You're not wrong. That's her rig and that's their driver. Michael, I'm not going in there."

"Of course you are. It has to happen sooner or later," he said. "You might as well get it over with."

"Michael," she said, trying hard to stop the sudden trembling that had begun at the sight of the Turner phaeton. "I don't know what you're talking about."

He took both her hands. "Did you really think she was through making trouble for you when she tried to take away Rose's baby?"

"But why?" she wailed. "What have I ever done to her?"

"I have my theories," he said. "But they're not important now. Come on, Darcy, I'll see you to the door."

"You're not coming in?"

"I'm not going in," he said firmly. "Believe me, I know what I'm doing."

As Darcy came in the door, Hildy came flying down the hall. There was fire in her eyes all right, but her lips were tight. She turned Darcy silently in the light, examining her critically. Then, after catching a loose curl and tucking it into place, she whispered fiercely, "That Turner woman is in there with your father."

"And Alex?" Darcy asked.

Hildy shook her head. "Just her. Best rap on the door," she said. "Your father's expecting you."

The captain called her name as she knocked, and she opened the door.

She could tell that he had been studying the specification sheets of various ship designs when he was interrupted. The blueprints were on the table at his side with his folded glasses on top of them. "Come in, my dear, and join Mrs. Turner and me."

Mrs. Turner, stiff in the rosewood chair, smiled warmly at him. "We've had a pleasant chat," she said, offering Darcy her hand. "I hope you had an invigorating walk?"

"I did, thank you," Darcy said.

Her father motioned her to bring a small stool from the hearth. "Come and sit by me, my dear."

Something in his voice frightened her, a heaviness that she hadn't heard since that first year after her mother's death.

She looked at him with concern as she seated herself by his side. He laid his hand on her shoulder and smiled. "Mrs. Turner was reviewing the reasons she felt it would be best for you to leave Galveston and go to Houston."

Mrs. Turner's voice rose in protest. "But, Captain Amos, I thought surely our conversation would remain confidential."

Darcy knew him well enough to recognize his mock surprise. "I don't see how it could be kept from Darcy when the subject was Darcy herself," he said smoothly. "You see, Mrs. Turner, I no longer think of Darcy as a child, willful or otherwise. She has worked as a team with Hildy these past few years to maintain my household. Together they kept it going through the horrid trial of the storm just past. When one performs as an adult, one should be granted adult privileges, don't you think?"

Mrs. Turner had stiffened with resentment. "Only within the bounds of convention."

"Convention," he repeated carefully. Then he took Darcy's hand. "I've never asked you this, Darcy, but where were you during the day and the night of the storm?"

So that was it. Not only had Mrs. Turner called her those names — her father would never use the term "willful" about her — but she had also repeated the same obscene suggestions that she had made to Darcy herself in the kitchen.

Darcy looked Mrs. Turner directly in the eye, not caring about the consequences. "I was with Michael Stephens," she said quietly.

"All through the storm?" her father asked.

She nodded. "We went to look for Rose but the orphanage was washed away. We drove to the wharf. I was worried about you. When I saw the *Sojourner* tied up and the cabin closed, we started home. We never made it."

"Where did you spend the night after turning down our invitation for safe shelter?" Mrs. Turner's tone was not pleasant.

"Please don't think I'm flippant, Papa, because this is the honest truth. Michael and I clung to whatever we could hang onto to stay afloat, a door, an iron fence, and finally a wall. For a long time we lodged in a great bank of flotsam only to be swept loose again. We ended the night in the branches of a salt cedar grove, neither of us knowing the other one had survived."

Her father's face had paled during this recital. When she stopped for breath, he leaned and caught her close with his good arm. "Oh, my dear," he said, his voice rough with emotion.

"It was Michael's stubborn strength that kept us alive," she told him.

"There was no reason for her to be out there *unchaperoned* with that young man," Mrs. Turner began. "Alex and I — "

Darcy's father shook his head. "That is not the point. Darcy *was* out there, and she and Michael survived an ordeal that destroyed almost six thousand lives. I resent your statement that her reputation is damaged by her being unchaperoned — in those circumstances — to such a degree that I should send her away from Galveston to be put under a 'strong hand,' as you so harshly put it."

"Harshly," she repeated angrily, rising. "I had only her eventual good in mind, Captain Dunlop." Although she was trembling, her voice stayed firm. "Given your attitude, and the direction in which this young woman is clearly headed, I will have to insist that your daughter terminate her friendship with my son."

Darcy stared at her and bit her lip to hold back her angry words. "As you will," Darcy's father said, nodding. "You will forgive me that I cannot rise and see you to the door."

Darcy would have escorted her out but Hildy was magically already there.

A long silence fell after the door closed behind her. Buffy, on the hearth, whined and nosed at Darcy's hand as she leaned, weeping, against her father's knee.

"That woman has a mind like a cesspool," Hildy said from the door.

"And a mouth to match," Darcy's father added. He lifted Darcy's face and wiped away her tears. "I forbid you to take her seriously."

"But the things she said. Oh, Papa, please don't send me away."

He shook his head. "That's the last thing I ever intend to do. If you want to go with your Aunt Julie, I will bid you good fortune. But do you believe that I would ever *send* my girl away? But you need to be sure, Darcy, very sure. Galveston will never be quite the same again."

"Neither will I," she told him. "This is my city, too. Mother, my friends, and my childhood are all buried on this island. Do you really mean the choice is mine to make?"

"Entirely," he said. "I want you to be happy, my dear."

Michael's words.

"I would never be happy away from you and Galveston," she said. "Never."

"Glad to hear that," he said with a low, comfortable chuckle. When she looked up at him in surprise, he added, "I was just amused that you made that decision without even knowing the rest of what Minnie Turner had to say."

"You mean, there was more?" Hildy said crossly from the doorway.

"You bet there was more," the captain said. "She and Alex are selling out — lock, stock and barrel — I think the expression is. They're going to settle in Houston, where she assured me she would be happy to oversee Darcy's upbringing as a devoted friend."

Darcy stared at him in horror, but Hildy broke into a cackle of laughter. "Things are looking up in this city already," she said.

"But will Rose and Aunt Julia understand?" Darcy asked when Hildy was gone.

He nodded. "Rose knows, and I imagine your Aunt Julia has already guessed."

Since her father looked tired after his emotional evening, and Hildy was openly yawning, Darcy went up the freshly mended stairs to her own bedroom. She lit a lamp and opened the shutters to lean on her windowsill. The moon was only slowly making its way across the night sky.

She had no idea how long Michael danced like a

crazy string puppet in the street before he caught her eye. His frantic signal scared her. Could something be wrong?

If nothing *was* wrong, what could be more shocking to convention than creeping out in the middle of the night like this to answer his summons? She felt like a thief letting herself out the back door so her father couldn't hear her from the parlor. She startled Michael when she appeared suddenly from behind the house.

Even that slender moon was enough to light his smile. She relaxed and rebuked him. "You seemed to be having a serious attack of something out here."

"Oh, I was," he said soberly. "I was literally dying of curiosity and impatience."

"Did you know what that woman was trying to do?" she asked him.

"I might have guessed," he said. "She had a long talk with Uncle and he nearly had a heart attack. She said she and Alex were leaving Galveston but, before she went, she wanted to warn him that you were no longer the kind of girl that Auntie would want Angela to associate with. She thought she would want to know so he could protect Angie."

Darcy gasped.

"Don't worry, Uncle handled it like a trooper. He said his and Auntie's true ambition had always been that Angie would be as fine a young lady as you. Then he showed her to the door and wished her well in Houston."

"But why, Michael, why is she so malicious toward me?"

"That's easy. Her precious Alex had set his heart on you for all the world to see. She had to break it up if it killed her."

Darcy shook her head. "Am I ever glad I won't have to live in the same town with her again!"

He was silent a moment. "You mean, you're staying here? You're not going to live with Rose and your aunt?"

"You knew I wouldn't leave Papa," she said. She shouldn't have to explain her decision to him. He had to realize that the only way she would have gone was if her father left, too. And he would never do that.

"Papa and I are family, a Galveston family. It would be like deserting a sinking ship for either of us to leave this city now. Anyway, Galveston will rise again," she assured him. "You wait and see."

"I intend to," he said quietly.

His words didn't register at once. She looked at him with his face half in shadow. How strange his tone had been, so very solemn but still with that hint of laughter behind it.

Suddenly his hands were on her shoulders. "Listen to me, Darcy. You didn't *hear* what I said. You're supposed to be happy that I changed my mind. I'm not leaving here any more than you are. I intend to be a part of seeing Galveston rise again."

She stared at him, giddy with joy and disbelief.

But all she could say was, "Michael, Michael," over and over.

He put his arms loosely around her and held her that way as he spoke. "You couldn't drive me away now, Darcy. This city is like a frontier with memories of past glory instead of just dreams. We begin with nothing except what we know it *can* be again."

She leaned against him, too happy to contain her own joy. She was certainly too happy to do more than half listen to all those grandiose engineering plans again. The details weren't important anyway. The important thing was that he was going to stay, and be a part of the rebuilding of the city and her own life. By the time he got to the part about raising the city, she was thinking back to the flood.

She didn't even realize that she was interrupting him when she spoke. "I owe you my life," she said suddenly.

He stared at her and laughed. "And I intend to claim it some day," he said. "And while we're at it, may I point out that it's impolite to break in like that? With a little practice you could be as rude as a Yankee."

"But I do, Michael," she said. "I really do owe you my life. How can I ever make it up to you?"

He held her very tightly. "You already have, Darcy. You've shown me a world I want to be a part of. With you in it, of course."

"I don't ever intend to leave," she told him.

He laughed. "After this city is back on its feet,

we can *both* take a good look at what we want to do."

She leaned her head against his shoulder, certain that she would never want to do anything with her life that didn't include Michael in it, Michael — brave and curious and golden.

And Yankee rude.